# Starshine

## and the Fanged Vampire Spider

D1052132

# Starshine

## and the Fanged Vampire Spider

by Ellen Schwartz

POLESTAR
An Imprint of Raincoast Books

Polestar Book Publishers and Raincoast Books acknowledge the ongoing support of The Canada Council; the British Columbia Ministry of Small Business, Tourism and Culture through the BC Arts Council; and the Government of Canada through the Book Publishing Industry Development Program (BPIDP).

Cover design by Les Smith.
Cover image by Ljuba Levstek.
Edited by Lynn Henry.

Printed and bound in Canada.

The author would like to thank James and Lynn Hill and the British Columbia Ministry of Government Sevices, Protocol and Events Branch.

Canadian Cataloguing in Publication Data

Schwartz, Ellen, 1949-
Starshine and the fanged vampire spider

ISBN 1-896095-60-7

I. Title.
PS8587.C578S82 2000          jC813'.54          C99-911336-4
PZ7.S407St 2000

Library of Congress Catalogue Number: 99-069299

Polestar Book Publishers/Raincoast Books
9050 Shaughnessy Street
Vancouver, BC
V6P 6E5

54321

*For all my nieces — and Josh.*

## Author's Note:

The *Araneus vampiricus*, or fanged vampire spider, is imaginary. I invented it to suit the purposes of the story. All other spiders mentioned in the book are real.

The Provincial Symbols mentioned in the story do exist, but there is no Provincial Arachnid and the method for adding a Provincial Symbol to the list is imaginary.

# Chapter One

Teachers just don't get it. They don't understand what field trips are for.

Kids get it. Every kid knows that field trips are for getting a day off school. They're for having fun, singing gross songs on the bus, eating junk food and feeling sorry for poor kids who are stuck at their desks, working.

My teacher, Ms. Fung, didn't get this.

There we were, my grade five class, standing on the steps outside the Royal British Columbia Museum in Victoria. So far the day had gone great. On the ferry over from Vancouver, my best friend, Julie Wong, and I had candy bars and pop for breakfast (which would make my mom, the original health food freak, blow her top if she knew). Then we stood on the outside deck and pretended we were being blown overboard, screaming, "Help! Help! Save me!" and after that we played video Checkers (I clobbered Julie). Meanwhile, other kids in our class were swapping lunches, horsing around in the toddler play area, chucking popcorn at one another and playing hide-and-seek in the cafeteria.

Then, on the bus ride down from the ferry terminal to Victoria, Tommy Scott started singing "Jimmy and Maggie sittin' in a tree, K-I-S-S-I-N-G," and Jimmy Tyler and Maggie Ralston turned red and started pounding on him. They came back with, "Tommy and Grace, sittin' in a tree ..." and Grace Ng said, "Don't make me puke!" She started in with, "Starshine and Sammy, sittin' in a tree ... " and I thought I'd die, because of course I don't like Sammy Dhaliwal — not like that — even though he's an OK kid, if you know what I mean. Sammy looked all embarrassed, too, so we started in on Julie and Mickey Rosen, and by the time we got to the museum, everybody was K-I-S-S-I-N-G everybody else, and the whole class was in hysterics.

We figured we'd hang around inside the museum for a while, then come outside and have a picnic lunch on the grass and maybe roam around downtown and buy tacky tourist souvenirs and get back on the bus and eat more junk on the ferry and have a perfectly wonderful day.

Then Ms. Fung spoiled it all.

She said, "Take out your notebooks and pencils, please. I have a very interesting assignment for you to do while you're in the museum."

Dead silence. Then:

"Assignment?"

"Aaaggghh!"

"Ms. Fung, you're ruining our day off!"

Ms. Fung looked shocked. "Day off? Since when is a field trip a day off?"

"Since forever," Sammy said. "It's … it's like a rule."

"I hate to break it to you, Sammy, but a field trip is not a day off. It's an opportunity for learning."

"But Ms. Fung, it's June," I wailed.

"So?"

"So school's almost over. We've worked all year. We deserve a break."

"A break from learning? I think not. Did you think we came all the way to the Royal British Columbia Museum just to goof off?"

"YES!" everybody yelled.

Ms. Fung levelled a look at the entire class. "Well, you thought wrong. Today, we're going to wrap up our unit on British Columbia with an assignment that will help you learn more about our province."

The class moaned. In unison.

Ms. Fung smiled. "Don't worry. It's a fun assignment."

She *really* didn't get it.

"Come on, now, pencils and notebooks."

To a chorus of sighs, there was a great unzipping of packs and rustling of papers.

"That's better. Now, we have spent the last month learning all about British Columbia. We've learned about the native people and the first settlers. The geography and the climate. The great rivers and the major cities. But we haven't learned everything there is to know. There must be something that each of you would like to know more about."

"Nope," Tommy said with an air of satisfaction. "Not one thing."

"Thomas," Ms. Fung intoned, "that was not a question. It was an order. Now, your assignment is to come up with a question. What else would you like to know about our province? Write it down. Then, while you're in the museum, find the answer, and write it down. Got that? All right. Write down your questions. I'll give you a minute to think."

There was a babble of whispers.

" … who cares?"

" … of all the nerve!"

"… there oughta be a law!"

But I wasn't complaining anymore. I didn't even mind having to do the assignment. Because the minute Ms. Fung had said, "something that you'd like to know about British Columbia," a question had popped into my head.

An important question. An exciting question: What is British Columbia's Provincial Arachnid?

There had to be one. There were all kinds of Provincial Symbols. We'd learned about them in our B.C. unit. Dogwood was the Provincial Flower. The Steller's Jay was the Provincial Bird. Our Social Studies book hadn't said anything about a Provincial Spider, but of course there was one. How could a province not have a Provincial Arachnid? Ridiculous.

And the Royal British Columbia Museum was certainly the right place to find out what it was.

I scribbled down the question, then showed it to Julie. She rolled her eyes. "Typical."

"What've you got?"

"How many beets are grown in B.C. every year?"

"What do you care about beets?"

"I don't," she said. "I was looking at Miranda's backpack and it made me think of beets."

I looked. Sure enough, Miranda's backpack was reddish-purple, just the colour of beets. "Julie," I said, "you've got a warped mind."

"You should talk," she said. "Provincial Arachnid. Who's warped here?" But she was smiling. We've been best friends for nearly two years. She understands how I feel about spiders.

Ms. Fung clapped her hands. "All right, I think we're ready to go in."

"Whoopee," Grace said sarcastically, and everybody laughed.

But not me. Now I couldn't wait to go in. Ms. Fung was right. This *was* a fun assignment!

Ms. Fung said we had an hour to find the answers to our questions. Then we were to meet in the lobby.

"Then can we have a picnic and go shopping and play frisbee?" Miranda Stockton asked.

Ms. Fung heaved a great sigh. "Would it be too much to expect you to keep your minds off food or songs or games or shopping for just one hour?"

"Yes!" the class chorused.

Ms. Fung shook her head. "Go, already."

We went, scattering in different directions. I dragged Julie over to a desk in the lobby, where a woman was sitting behind a sign that said ASK ME.

She greeted me with a smile. "Can I help you?"

"Sure," I said. "Where can I find out about the Provincial Arachnid?"

Her smile faltered. "The Provincial what?"

"You know, like the Provincial Flower and the Provincial Bird and stuff like that."

Her smile came back. "Oh, you mean the Provincial Symbols. There's a beautiful display in the Chamber of Provincial Symbols. Straight down this hall, past the Seashore exhibit, turn left, and you can't miss it."

"Thanks." I turned to Julie. "Please can we do mine first?"

"Sure. You think I'm in a big hurry to find out about beets?"

A colourful mural took up nearly the whole wall. I could read the title clear across the room:

## BEAUTIFUL BRITISH COLUMBIA
## OUR PROVINCIAL SYMBOLS

I was so excited. Would it be the fanged vampire spider? Would it be the trapdoor spider? Or the wolf spider?

All of a sudden I couldn't look. I was too excited. I turned my back to the mural and said, "Jule, just tell me what it is, OK?"

She crossed the room. I waited. Silence.

"Jule," I said impatiently.

"There isn't any," she said, then burst out laughing. "Oh, I don't believe it! Starshine, there's a Provincial Tartan."

"What?" I spun around.

"Honest. I guess it's for making official kilts." Laughing, she clicked her heels in a little highland dance.

"Julie," I said in a threatening voice, "the Provincial Arachnid. What is it?"

"I told you, there isn't one. But look," — she laughed again — "we've got an Official Mineral Emblem — jade. Now, what on earth does B.C. need an Official Mineral Emblem for?"

I ran over to the mural. There was the Provincial Flag, with the sun rising into wavy blue stripes. The Provincial Coat of Arms, with a deer on one side and a mountain sheep on the other. The Provincial Bird — Steller's Jay — deep blue with a punk-rock spiky black head. The Provincial Flower — Dogwood — white petals on green leaves. The Provincial Tree — Western Red Cedar — green and brown, a too-perfect tree, like kids draw. The Provincial Mineral Emblem — Jade — milky-green, cool and smooth. The Provincial bloody Tartan — a plaid of blue, white, green, red and gold.

No Provincial Arachnid.

How could this be? How could British Columbia not have a Provincial Spider?

I read the mural all over again, searching for a clue. It said that the Pacific Dogwood was adopted as B.C.'s floral emblem in 1956, the Western Red Cedar became the Official Tree in 1988, and the Steller's Jay was voted the most popular bird by the people of British Columbia in 1987.

A light went on in my head. A shiver went up my back. "Julie," I said.

She was still giggling about the Provincial Tartan. "Ah yes, my wee lassie, what can I do for ye?" she said in a Scottish accent. (Julie's really good at accents. She's going to be an actress when she grows up.)

"There's no Provincial Arachnid, right?"

"Right."

"And that's wrong, right?"

"Wrong? Right?"

I gave her a look. "You know what I mean."

"Well … yeah, I guess."

"After all, any province that has an Official Mineral Emblem and a Provincial Tartan should have a Provincial Arachnid, right?"

She gave me an uneasy look. "Starshine, where are you going with this?"

"I mean, it's not like tartans do any good for the province. They just sit there, looking plaid. But spiders do lots of good. They eat insects. They provide food for birds. They produce amazing chemicals that paralyze and dissolve their food."

"But Star —"

"And spiders' silk is so amazing. It's even stronger than parachute rope, for its size and weight."

"Yeah, but —"

"And British Columbia is loaded with great spiders. Nursery web spiders. Wolf spiders. Burrowing spiders. Fanged vampire spiders." I was all excited now. "Julie, what this province needs is a Provincial Arachnid. And I'm going to give it one!"

"You're what? Star, you're cracked."

I ignored that. "Which one do you think it should be? Garden spiders are the most common species, but they're — well, I hate to say it — boring. Trapdoor spiders are neat. They hide in a tunnel in the ground. They cover the entrance with a sheet of silk. When they feel an insect going by — POW! — they spring out and catch it. But there's not a lot of them in B.C. You couldn't really say they *represent* B.C., if you know what I mean —"

"Star —"

"Maybe the fanged vampire spider would be better. *Araneus vampiricus*. Remember I told you how I found one at camp last summer, after everybody thought they were extinct?" I tried to sound modest. "That was so cool, if I do say so myself. Yeah, Jule, the more I think about it, the more I think the *Araneus vampiricus* is the right choice. They're beautiful. They're harmless. Best of all, they eat slugs —"

"Starshine!" Julie shouted.

A guard glared at us. "Quiet, please."

"Star," she said in a lower voice, "you can't just wave your arm and say, 'I hereby declare that the whatchama-whosit is British Columbia's Provincial Arachnid.' You're not an official person. You're just a kid. Probably the government has to do it. The Premier or somebody like that."

"No, Jule, that's the great thing. Look." I pointed to the mural. "'Adopted in 1988. Adopted in 1956.' The Steller's Jay was voted the most popular bird. See?"

"See what?"

"The people chose. If they could choose a bird, why not a spider? These symbols were adopted. So why can't a Provincial Arachnid be adopted, too? There's a way to do it — we just have to find out how. And we will."

"We? Did you say *we*?"

I put both my hands on Julie's shoulders. "Jule," I said, "I'm going to make the fanged vampire spider British Columbia's Provincial Arachnid. But I can't do it alone. I'll need your help."

For a moment, Julie looked doubtful. Then she broke into a grin. "Hey, kiddo, when have I ever let you down?"

On the ferry home, Ms. Fung collected our questions and answers. I told her I hadn't been able to find the answer to mine. "I hope you won't flunk me," I said. "I tried, really I did. You can ask Julie. There just isn't a Provincial Arachnid."

"That's all right, Starshine," she said. "You thought of a good question, and you found the answer."

"But that's not all," I said, and told her about my plan to make the fanged vampire spider the Provincial Arachnid. "I've got to tell you, Ms. Fung," I said, "when you first said we had to do school work, I was really ticked off. I mean, really, Ms. Fung — on a field trip! But I'm glad you did, because if you hadn't, I never would have thought of that question and I never would have found out the awful truth and I never would have taken on this great project. Just think, Ms. Fung, British Columbia is going to have a Provincial Arachnid — all because you gave us that stupid assignment. Thanks!"

Ms. Fung looked confused. "You're welcome," she said. "I think."

# Chapter Two

A few days later, I was sitting on the bus. Looking out the window, I saw Glynnis.

Glynnis was as big as a building.

I yelled, "Glynnis!" and hopped off the bus.

I got grounded.

Now, I know that sounds nuts, but I swear it's true. I'll explain.

This was the very first time I'd taken the bus all by myself. It was a big deal. A very big deal. I was taking the bus from school to the dentist. Straight down Main Street from 33rd to 14th. No problem, right?

You do not know my mom. My mom was freaked out. Of course, it was her fault that I had to take the bus in the first place, because she couldn't take me to the dentist. She was putting up a show of her stuff at this art gallery on Granville Island called Goddess Grove — my mom's a potter, and lately she's been making clay goddesses — and the opening was that night and she had to be at the gallery all afternoon. And my dad was busy making this huge window for some rich people who live in a fancy house on the other side of Vancouver — he's a stained glass artist — so he couldn't take me either. So I had to take the bus.

I had assured my mom I would be fine, but she's the nervous type. I don't know what she was worried about. Probably that I would be kidnapped, or I would suddenly forget how to read street signs and miss my stop, or I would get bus-sick and throw up on the person next to me, or some other silly thing that only moms can think of.

But there was no other way for me to get to the dentist. So there I was, sitting on the bus, happily watching the street signs go by ... 28th ... 27th ... watching a cute little round-faced baby drool ... 24th ... 23rd ... watching a green-haired punk rocker thrash around to screeching earphones ... 21st ... 20th ... when I looked out the window, and there was Glynnis.

Now, Glynnis is one of my friends from Camp Crescent Moon, where I went last summer. Where I found the fanged vampire spider. Glynnis is one of my favourite people in the whole world. She's the queen of corny jokes. Like: "What do you call a carpenter who misplaces his tools?" "A saw loser." And that's one of her good ones.

So you can imagine how excited I was to see her. We hadn't

seen each other since last July, and here it was June already, almost a year. Glynnis lives in Victoria and I live in Vancouver. We'd meant to get together during the year, but somehow it had never happened.

The only problem was, Glynnis was on a billboard. A huge billboard at the side of the street, the kind with panels that keep changing. So, one minute there was Glynnis, larger than life ... and then she turned into a red convertible driven by a sexy babe in a low-cut dress ... and then the car turned into a diaper ad with a huge, half-naked, toothless, smiling baby ... and then there was Glynnis again.

Glynnis's billboard said — I caught it the second time around — CEREBRAL PALSY. HELP THE CHILDREN. PLEASE GIVE GENEROUSLY. And there was Glynnis, with her crutches and braces, and her short brown hair, and her big green eyes, and her shy smile.

I couldn't believe it. Not that Glynnis would be chosen to be on a CP billboard, but that she'd let herself be put on one. It's just not a Glynnis thing to do. She's too shy. I just couldn't picture her agreeing to let her face be blown up and plastered on a billboard for everyone to see.

But there she was. I was so stunned, I yelled, "Glynnis!" and hopped off the bus. I stood on the sidewalk, staring up at the billboard, watching the picture change, waiting for Glynnis to come around again, getting a crick in my neck, saying intelligent things like, "Glynnis, is it really you?" and hollering to everyone who walked by, "I know her! I know her!"

By the time I'd had enough of staring at Glynnis and realized where I was — 20th Avenue — I ran the rest of the way to 14th Avenue. I was panting when I burst into the dentist's office, twenty minutes late. The receptionist had already called my dad at home and my dad had called my mom at the gallery and my mom nearly had a heart attack and was convinced that I'd either been kidnapped or misread the street signs or got bus-sick, and she was on the verge of calling the police. And that's why I got grounded.

"Glynnis!" I said over the phone, "I saw you!"

"You did? Where?"

"On the side of a building. Near my dentist's office."

"What? — Oh." She sounded embarrassed. "Are those posters up already?"

"Those are no posters, Glynnis. They're billboards. They're huge. You're huge."

"Oh no."

"You look good."

She groaned.

"Really, you do. But what are you doing on a billboard?"

"Oh, Starshine, it's so embarrassing. You see, the CCPA — "

"The CP — what?"

"Canadian Cerebral Palsy Association."

"Oh. OK, go on."

"Well, they asked me if I'd be this year's poster child. I don't know why. Probably they'd already asked everybody else, and everybody else had had the sense to say no. I mean, who wants their face plastered all over posters and billboards and — God, Starshine, was it really on the side of a building?"

"It was against a building. You know, one of those billboards with the pictures that change? You were one of the ads. You kept changing into other things."

"Like what?"

"First a sports car and then diapers."

"Diapers? Great — me and babies' bums." She laughed. "Well, anyway, they asked me and at first I said no. But then the photographer came to see me, this guy Tony, and he had this little dog, Stumpy. He was missing a leg — Stumpy, that is, not Tony — that was why he was called Stumpy. One back leg was cut off about halfway and he just had this stump. And he was so cute, he gave a little hop and a lurch with every step. And he could do everything, just like a regular dog, go up stairs, go down stairs, hoppity-lurch, hoppity-lurch. And he really liked me — he came right over and licked my hand and then he licked my crutches and looked up at me as if to say, 'We're in the same boat, aren't we?' 'cause I lurch, too. And I just — oh, I don't know, Star, before I knew what I was doing, I said yes, I'd be the poster child. And now my stupid face is on the side of buildings." She groaned again.

"But you look good, Glynnis. Large, but good."

She laughed. "They haven't gone up in Victoria yet. I hope they never do. I don't want to see my nose as big as a house!"

"It's only as big as a couch," I said. "Or maybe an easy chair."

"That sure makes me feel better." She laughed again. "So, you going back to camp?"

"No."

"What? Why not? Ruth wasn't that mad at you."

I laughed too. Ruth was the director of Camp Crescent Moon. Last summer I'd gotten into a heap of trouble — and the whole rest of my cabin-mates with me — for sneaking out after dark and spying on our counsellor, Joey — that's short for Joelle — and her boyfriend, Todd. And we would've pulled it off too, only right in the middle of our spy operation, I happened to discover that *Araneus vampiricus*, which I'd been searching for all summer. When I saw it, I made a little bit of noise. Well, I hollered, actually, and we all got caught and Ruth grounded us big-time. (Now that I think of it, I get grounded a lot.)

"No, it's not that," I said. "My grandma's having an operation and we're going to Montreal to take care of her, right when camp is."

"Can't she have it during the boys' session?" Glynnis asked.

"I already tried that."

"Fooey."

"Are the others going?" I asked.

"Roxanne is — of course. Frannie and Priya, too."

"Miranda, too," I said. "That's everybody, then — except me."

"It won't be the same without you, Star."

We both sighed. Then I shouted, "Glynnis, I've got a brilliant idea!"

"Uh-oh."

I laughed. "Not like that one. My birthday is next week but I was going to wait until school lets out to have my party. Why don't I make it a sleep-over and everybody from Half Moon Cabin can come?"

"That *is* brilliant."

"Would your parents bring you over?"

"If I whine enough. And clean my room."

I looked at the calendar and we picked the first Saturday after school ended.

"See you soon."

"Can't wait."

Frannie shrieked, "Heek, heek!"

Frannie has a weird laugh. It's half a shriek and half the kind of noise you make when you're laughing so hard you can't catch your breath and you gasp in air — well, that's the best I can do. You really have to hear it.

Anyway, when I told Frannie about my sleep-over she got so excited she started laughing and heek-heeking all over the place. Then I really missed her, 'cause I hadn't heard her weird laugh in such a long time, and tears came to my eyes and I nearly started crying. But then I thought what an idiot I was to be crying, and that made me laugh, and I opened my mouth and out came a sound that was halfway between a laugh and a cry. It sounded like, "Squawk!"

"Heek-heek!"

"Squawk!"

"What?"

"Squawk!"

"Starshine, are you OK?"

"Squawk!"

"Starshine, what's the matter? Are you dying? Don't die."

I roared with laughter.

"Starshine, what's going on? Say something!"

"I — I — " I was laughing too hard to speak. "I — God, I miss you, Frannie."

"Is that all? Geez, I thought you were croaking on me."

"Just digging your crazy laugh."

"*My* crazy laugh. You sounded like a chicken getting strangled, Starshine."

I started laughing all over again, and so did Frannie, and soon she was heek-heeking away, and my stomach was hurting from laughing so hard, so finally I said, "See you at my party, Frannie," and we hung up.

Priya said, "Thank you, Starshine, I would be very happy to come."

Priya's very polite and proper. At camp, she was the most polite and proper one of us. (Except Miranda, of course, but that's another story. Miranda was probably born proper. When she was a baby, she probably said, "Mother, may I wet my diaper?" Of course, she was a little less proper by the end of camp, by the time I got through with her — but that's another story, too.)

Priya isn't like that. Not prissy, just shy. Very shy. But not a goody-goody, either. At camp, she wasn't known for thinking up bad things to do — I think I can modestly claim that honour — but once I thought of them, she didn't have any trouble joining in.

Like the time I came up with the idea of sneaking down to the lake after dark. No one else would go with me except Priya. But boy, did we have fun. We swam in the moonlight and jumped like Tarzan on the rope swing, and it was so neat, just the two of us and the inky black water and the shadowy cattails and the cool grass. We climbed up the hill to the rope swing over and over until our legs would hardly hold us anymore, and splashed each other, and shrieked as loud as we wanted under the big round moon. And we would've gotten away with it, too, only Miranda tattled on us and we got — you guessed it — grounded. Boy, I could have killed her. But then — well, let's just say things worked out. Yet another story.

"I can't wait for camp to start, can you?" Priya said. "Do you think Joey'll be our counselor again?"

"I hate to tell you this, Priya, but I'm not going this summer."

"What? Why not?"

I explained about my grandma.

"But Starshine, you've got to! Who will think of naughty things to do?"

"You'll just have to take over for me, Priya."

"No one can take over for you, Starshine. You have the best bad ideas."

I laughed. "I wish I could go. Believe me, I had a huge fight with my parents."

She sighed. "It won't be the same without you. Me and Frannie and Glynnis and Roxanne and Miranda — and no Starshine."

I didn't tell her I'd pictured exactly that — all my camp friends together, without me. "You'll have fun," I said, trying not to sound jealous. "And we'll have fun at my sleep-over, too. It'll be like a mini-camp. All us Half-Mooners."

"Just like old times, eh?" she said.

"Hey, kiddo, what's shakin'?" Roxanne said. She talks like that, honest. She also shouts. I had to hold the phone about a foot away from my head.

"A sleep-over. Can you come?"

"Can't wait, it's a date."

I had to laugh. "What's new?"

"Tell you what's new, Suzy-Q. I'm taking guitar lessons."

"Really? How's it going?"

"Great! So far I can play 'Hound Dog' and 'Don't Be Cruel.' Want to hear?"

"That's all right," I began but there was a crash as the phone fell. A minute later I heard a bon-n-n-g-g-g as a guitar bashed into something.

"Are you there?" Roxanne shouted.

"I'm here."

"OK. Just a minute. Hold on — " Bash. Thump. Strum — flat. "It's a little out of tune. I'm not so good at tuning."

No kidding.

Lots of fast strumming noise. "You ain't nothin' but a hound dawg, cryin' all the tahm ..." Screech. Long pause. I thought she was gone but then — strum, very flat. "No, that's not it. Hold on ... " Strum — sharp. "No ... darn it, where does that finger go? Oh, yeah ... " Strum — a note. Not the right note, but a note. "You ain't never caught a rabbit and you —" First chord — flat. "— ain't no friend of mahn." Lots of fast strumming. Big finish. "There! How was that?"

"That was — well, Roxanne, I don't know what to say."

"That good, huh?"

I just mumbled.

"Hey, I'll bring my guitar to your party. Won't that be the cat's meow?"

So it was arranged. All my friends from camp were coming to my party. Plus Julie, of course. I couldn't wait.

There was only one problem. My camp friends all knew each other. We'd lived together for three weeks. We'd gotten into trouble together. We'd shared jokes and stories. We were all buddies — all except Julie.

Julie didn't know anybody who was going to be at the party, except me — and Miranda, who was in our class at school. But Miranda would probably hang out with the camp friends. Which meant that Julie would be left out. The rest of us would be laughing and remembering stuff from camp and Julie wouldn't be able to join in. I remembered feeling that way on the bus up to camp last summer — sitting and listening to a bunch of "old-timers" laughing and telling stories that only they could share. I'd felt left out. Jealous.

Well, that wasn't going to happen to my best friend. I wouldn't let it. I'd do something — I didn't know what, but something — to make sure that Julie was part of things. That she was included.

What was it she'd said to me the other day at the museum? "When have I ever let you down?" Well, I'd do the same for her. After all, what were best friends for?

# Chapter Three

How do you get a spider named the Provincial Arachnid?

I started by calling the Premier of British Columbia, Jack Sherman. Of course, I didn't actually talk to *him*. I talked to someone in his office, probably the fifth assistant to the seventh secretary. He told me to call my Member of the Legislative Assembly. So I did. She suggested I call the Provincial Archives. The Provincial Archivist sent me to the Provincial Mapmaker. The Provincial Mapmaker directed me to the Fish and Wildlife Branch. "Why don't you try the Premier's office?" they suggested.

Aarrgghh!

Finally I ended up with Protocol and Events, whatever that was. "Protocol and Events, good morning. Who's calling?" said a woman's voice.

"Starshine Shapiro."

"*Starshine Shapiro*? Is that your real name?"

"Yes," I snapped. Boy, do I ever get sick of getting teased about my name.

"You lucky duck!" she said. "I'd kill for a name like that."

"Y-you would?"

"Yeah!"

"You mean it?"

"Sure, I mean it. What a great name. Such personality."

"Gee ... " I said, "what's your name?"

"Jane Smith."

"Are you kidding? You know how much I've always wanted a nice plain name like Jane Smith?"

"Nice! Boring, you mean. My parents had absolutely no imagination."

"Mine had too much."

"Trade you."

"You're on!"

"Wish we could," she said with a laugh. "Now, Starshine Shapiro, what can I do for you?"

I explained.

"It's really quite simple," she said. "First, you have to write up a petition saying that the *Ar*-uh-"

"*Araneus vampiricus.*"

"Right. That it should be B.C.'s Provincial Arachnid."

"OK." Easy, I thought, and wrote down, Petition.

"Then you have to get three thousand people to sign it."

"Right." I wrote 3,000.

*Three thousand?*

"And then you bring the petition to my office and we check it and then it goes to Parliament and then the Members of the Legislative Assembly vote and then the — your spider — is proclaimed the Provincial Arachnid by the Premier. And then there's a ceremony at the Royal British Columbia Museum, in the Chamber of Provincial Symbols, to make it official."

I put down my pencil. I didn't say anything.

"Starshine, you there?"

"Three thousand signatures?" I said. "Are you kidding? I might as well forget the whole thing right now."

"Hey, that's no attitude," Jane said. "You can't give up before you even start."

"But three thousand is so many —"

"Yes, it is. It's a heck of a lot. So you've got to convince people. Convince me. Why should the *Araneus vampiricus* be named B.C.'s official arachnid?"

"Well, it's beautiful, for one thing," I said. "It's got black fangs — that's why it's called the fanged vampire spider — and red and yellow stripes on its back."

"OK. Good-lookin'. What else?"

"Well, everybody thought the *Araneus vampiricus* was extinct, but then I found one, up on the Sunshine Coast, and arachnologists all over the world went nuts. They swarmed to B.C., and ever since they've been finding lots of them. It turns out that the *Araneus vampiricus* was hibernating all those years — that's why no one saw any — and that's totally amazing, 'cause it's the first case of spider hibernation ever heard of, and no one knows why they do it. It's a huge mystery in the spider world."

"OK. Mysterious. What else?"

"Well, they eat slugs...."

"WHAT!" She yelled so loud, I nearly dropped the phone.

"I said they eat slugs."

"I heard you, I heard you. Slugs! That is amazing. I hate slugs. Can I get a few of these things for my garden? Slugs! Everybody'll sign when they hear that. Everybody who's ever had slugs eat their way through their broccoli."

"You think so?"

"I know so."

"But three thousand people? How will I ever find three thousand people?"

"You'll figure it out."

"I will?"

"Sure. I have faith in you. And good luck, Starshine."

Thanks a lot, I thought, and dialed Julie's number. I told her we had to collect three thousand signatures.

"Holy smokes," she said. "Sounds impossible."

"But Julie, we've got to do it. B.C. needs a Provincial Arachnid."

"Yeah, but how?"

"I don't know."

We sat there in gloomy silence. Then Julie said, "Let's sleep on it, OK? Maybe one of us will get a brainstorm."

"OK," I said doubtfully.

"I know something that'll cheer you up," she said in a mischievous tone.

"What?"

"What I'm getting you for your birthday."

"What?"

"Nice try." She laughed. "You'll love it. You'll really love it."

"Julie!"

She laughed again. "I can't wait for your party." Then, a little hesitantly, "Do you think your camp friends'll like me, Star?"

"Of course!"

"I just wondered."

"Don't worry about it, Jule. It'll be fine."

We hung up. The moment I put the phone down, I got a brainstorm. My party. Of course. Glynnis and Roxanne and Priya and Frannie and Miranda. That was five. Plus Julie and me, made seven. A small army. I'd get them to help. The seven of us would fan out, pound the streets, gather signatures, sign up everyone we knew. Together we could do it.

I nearly picked up the phone and called Julie back, but I stopped. It would be more fun to announce it at my party. After dessert, after presents, right before bed. "Guys," I'd say, "I need your help." And of course they'd all say yes.

"Starshine!"

"Glynnis!"

"Priya!"

"Starshine!"

"Roxanne!"

"Frannie!"

"Heek-heek!"

"Miranda!"

We stood in my front hall, hugging and laughing in a crush of sleeping bags and pillows, overnight bags, Roxanne's guitar case and my birthday presents.

"You're taller, Star."

"You're not, Frannie."

"Oh, shush."

"Hey, look at my guitar, guys. I'll play you a concert. So far I know three songs. Well, two and a half."

"Let me guess, Roxanne. Elvis?"

"Of course!"

"Glynnis, I saw you! On the side of the bank."

"Aarrgghh! Don't remind me. That subject is off limits this weekend. Everybody got that? Off limits!"

"Anybody heard from Joey?"

"I did."

"She still going with Todd?"

"Hot and heavy."

"Whoo-hoo!"

"Boomba, boomba, boomba," Roxanne chanted, and we all laughed.

Last summer, we'd been teasing Joey about making out with Todd, and Roxanne had invented a new way of kissing — by bumping behinds. Now, we all joined in, smashing bums together. "Boomba, boomba, boomba!"

Then I noticed Julie.

She was standing off to the side, watching. Totally left out.

I could have kicked myself. I'd promised I wouldn't let this happen, and here I was, reminiscing with my camp friends, laughing at memories that only we shared.

I yelled for quiet. When the uproar died down, I swept my arm to the side. "Guys, may I present … Julie."

"Julie!" they all cried, and rushed over to her.

"So you're the famous Julie."

"You were Athena in the play, right?"

"I heard you're such a great actress."

"Do an accent for us. Please?"

A shy smile spread over Julie's face at the same time that a blush pinked her cheeks. She looked at me as if to say, You told them about me?

Of course I did, I beamed back in my smile. You're my best friend, aren't you?

She turned to them with a grin. "Which ehk-cent would you like, mites?" she said in a perfect Australian drawl.

Everything was going great. For one thing, Peggy wasn't home.

Peggy's my little sister. She's four and a half. She's a pain. She's also very cute. Too cute. She always steals the show. So it was very good that she was having dinner at her new best friend Kirsten's house.

For another thing, my mom and dad were leaving us alone.

My mom was in her studio, working on some new goddesses. Paulie, the owner of Goddess Grove, loved her Indian series — Lakshmi, the goddess of prosperity, and Sarasvati, the goddess of knowledge — and had asked for more. So my mom was starting a Chinese series. She was hard at work on Kuan Yin, the goddess of compassion.

My dad, meanwhile, was in the kitchen, making pizza and whistling. My dad whistles all the time. Lately he's been into musicals. Today it was *My Fair Lady*. The strains of "Wouldn't It Be Loverly?" floated out of the kitchen along with the delicious smell of pizza sauce.

Best of all, Julie was fitting in with everybody. Priya had brought a bottle of black nail polish, and Julie painted Glynnis's nails and Glynnis painted hers. They were giggling away like old friends. Then Roxanne brought out her guitar and Julie joined in as we belted out "You Ain't Nothin' But a Hound Dog" at the top of our lungs — mainly to drown out the sound of Roxanne's guitar playing. Then Frannie grabbed her pillow and shoved it over Roxanne's face before she could start another song, and the next thing I knew, pillows were flying everywhere, and Julie was bashing everybody and getting bashed right back, just like she was one of the gang. While she was turning to avoid Priya's pillow, she flashed me a grin, and I flashed one back at her, as if to say, See, I told you everything would be OK.

"Dinner is served," my dad announced just as the pillow fight was over. Everybody was starved, so we all trooped into the kitchen and had three slices apiece of his vegetarian pizza.

He beamed and whistled "I'm Getting Married in the Morning."

I felt like whistling, too. This was the best party I'd ever had. Next we'd have dessert, and then I'd open my presents, and then I'd tell my friends about the fanged vampire spider project and get six helpers. What more could I ask for?

After we'd eaten, Priya said, "Now what?"

I grinned. "We're going out."

"Out where?"

"Just out," I said, trying to sound mysterious. Actually, we were going to the Ice Cream Pagoda for dessert instead of having birthday cake. This was a surprise — I hadn't even told Julie.

The Ice Cream Pagoda is the greatest ice cream parlour in the world. Or at least in Vancouver. It's a couple of blocks away. It's long and narrow, with ice cream bins all down one wall, and usually there's a crowd lined up down the other wall. It's owned by this Chinese family, the Hings, and about ten members of the family are always in there, from babies to the old, old grandpa. He must be around a hundred and he's all bent over and wears black cotton slippers and kind of shuffles around, but he knows me and always gives me a toothless smile and lots of tastes in tiny plastic spoons.

They have about 82 flavours of ice cream, all these weird ones like chili and black bean and ginseng. I mean, they have regular flavours, too, but it's more fun to try the weird ones. And the funny thing is, they're good. Honest. This time, I was planning to try salsa.

"OK," Glynnis said, "just let me get my crutches."

"And my sunglasses! I can't go out without my genuine Elvis Presley sunglasses," Roxanne cried, putting on a pair of pointy-framed, rhinestone-studded shades.

I got money from my dad for everybody's cones. "Ready?" I said.

"Ready," they all shouted.

I opened the front door — and in ran Peggy.

And that's when the trouble started.

# Chapter Four

(Drum roll.) *Ladies and gentlemen, it's the Peggy Shapiro Show!* ( Cheering and whistling.) *Watch the world's cutest four-year-old steal the party right out from under the nose of the birthday girl!* (Wild applause.) *And here's the star of our show, Peggy Shapiro!*

Peggy ran in. As soon as she spotted my friends, she put on her cute look. Like a mask. I saw it happen, like I've seen it so many times before. It only took a second, but there it was. Her little button nose scrunched up, her chubby cheeks puffed out. She cocked her head and one stubby pigtail pointed up and the other pointed down, and she grinned her aren't-I-adorable grin and said, "Hi, party people!"

Everyone ran over to her. Like she was a magnet. One minute they were standing by me; the next, they were standing by her. Vroom. There they go. Just like always. That's the Peggy Shapiro Show.

"You must be Peggy."

"Isn't she cute?"

"Precious!"

"How old are you, Peggy?"

She held up four fingers and crooked her thumb.

"Oh, she means four and a half. Isn't she clever?"

Roxanne tickled Peggy under the chin and Peggy squealed and ran behind me, peeking out to see if Roxanne was coming after her. So cute. She's not even ticklish under the chin.

"Isn't she adorable?"

"I wish I had a little sister," Frannie said.

She's yours, I thought. Absolutely free.

Meanwhile, Priya was staring at Peggy with a confused look. "I've seen her before, I'm sure of it," she murmured to Frannie. "But where?"

"You know, I was thinking the same thing," Frannie said. "I can't figure it out."

Just then Peggy pulled a pipe-cleaner cat out of her backpack. "Look at my kitty," she said proudly. "I made it at Kirsten's. Meowww..."

Everybody ooohed and aahed.

"I know!" Priya cried. "The Kitten Krunchies Girl."

"That's it!" Frannie said.

"Who's the Kitten Krunchies Girl?" Glynnis asked.

Peggy looked at her in amazement. "Don't you watch TV?" she said, and informed Glynnis that she was the star of a whole series of television commercials featuring Kitten Krunchies cat food, Biskittens (cat-shaped biscuits), Kitty-Vites (cat vitamins) and Kitten Kritters (catnip-stuffed cat toys). And then she trotted out all her stuff: the silver Kitten Krunchies jacket, the Biskittens baseball cap, the lunch box, the mug, all with her face plastered on them.

"Gee willikers," Roxanne said, "you're famous. Can I have your autograph?" She produced a piece of paper and a pencil, and Peggy, her tongue sticking out of the corner of her mouth, printed P E G G Y.

"Wow!" Roxanne said when Peggy presented it to her. "I'll keep it with my Elvis Presley baseball card collection and my miniature Graceland statue and my replica Elvis Presley toothbrush."

Peggy beamed.

"Well, that's just great," I said, "but we really should get going, guys."

Peggy looked up. "Where you goin', Star?"

"Out."

"Where out?"

"Just out."

"I want to come."

"No."

"But Star, I want to be with you." This was one of her favourite lines.

"No."

"I'll give you ten kisses!"

Now, that would really make me change my mind. "No."

"But Star, you're my best sister."

"I'm your only sister. Besides, this is just for big girls."

"I'm big! I'm very big!"

Her voice rose and my mom and dad came over. I could see that my friends were uneasy. They could tell something unpleasant was coming. They were right.

"What's the matter, Peggy?" my dad asked.

"I want to go with Star." She already had tears in her eyes.

"Oh, no," my mom said, "this is Star's party."

"But I want to —"

"This is just for Star and her friends," my dad added. "A special treat."

Wrong choice of words.

"*I* want a special treat!"

"But Peggy —"

"I *really, really* want a special treat!" Her lower lip trembled.

You know how you can see a tornado coming? At first the big black cloud is far away, but then it gets bigger and closer and blacker? That's how it is with Peggy. The lower-lip-tremble is the distant warning. Before you can take cover, the storm is on you.

Right on cue, she burst into tears, threw herself on the floor and started kicking.

"Now, you stop that, Peggy," my mom said, trying to sound strict.

Louder crying. Harder kicking. "I wanna go, I wanna go, I wanna go."

My friends gathered around. They were staring at Peggy in amazement. I guess temper tantrums weren't part of their everyday lives.

"There's no need for this, Peggy," my dad said.

"But I'll be a good girl," Peggy wailed. Amazing how she can think of these arguments in the middle of flailing around.

"I'm sorry, Peggy —"

Heart-rending sobs. "But I love Star!"

Yeah, right. I love her so much, I don't want her to have fun without me.

Now she was gasping for breath. My mom leaned closer. "Peggy?" she said in a concerned voice.

My dad knelt down. "Peggy!" he said, putting his ear to her chest to make sure she was still breathing.

Why do they always fall for this?

Checking out of the corner of her eye to make sure they were watching, Peggy gasped harder. She sounded like she was going to expire on the spot.

"Speak to me, Pumpkin," my dad said.

Peggy wheezed. Too distressed to speak, poor thing.

"Peggy, it's all right, honey, just stop crying, it's not good for you to get so upset," my mom said, gathering Peggy into her arms. Peggy gave a fresh sob, then lay limp. "Oh, Pumpkin, it's all right, really it is, just calm down, nice deep breaths, that's it."

Peggy gave a piteous sigh. The poor tyke would live, but her heart was broken.

My mom and dad exchanged a look. I knew that look. So did Peggy. A tiny smile twitched her mouth. My mom and dad didn't see it because they were looking up at me. Shame-faced. Desperate.

"We know it's your party, Star … " my mom began.

"And we know we said you didn't have to take her … "

"But she's so upset … "

"And it's only for a few minutes … "

"Just this one little thing … "

I glared at them. This was totally unfair and they knew it, and I knew it, and Peggy even knew it. I started to say, "No w —" but Julie put her hand on my arm.

"It's OK, Star, let her come."

"Yeah," Roxanne said, "no problemo."

"We don't mind," Miranda said. "Do we, guys?"

There was murmured agreement. Chickens, I thought. They just wanted the tantrum to end.

Peggy gazed with tear-filled eyes at the faces around her, hopefully, yearningly. Triumphantly.

I know when I'm beaten.

"Oh, all right," I said crossly.

"Yay!" Peggy jumped to her feet.

"You'd better be a good girl, Pumpkin," my mom said, wagging her finger.

"I will!" Tears all gone. Miraculous.

"And hold Star's hand all the way there and all the way back."

"I will!"

"And go straight to bed when you get home."

"I will!"

My dad leaned close to me. "Thanks, Star. We owe you, big-time."

"You're not kidding," I muttered, then turned toward the others. "OK, everybody, let's go."

Everyone moved toward the door.

"Wait!" Peggy called. "I got to get my sweatshirt. In case I get cold."

"Peggy, it's sweltering out there."

"You never know, Star." She ran to her room and came back with her sweatshirt, the blue one with pink and yellow cats on it and COOL CAT on the back. "You like my sweat-shirt?" she asked Frannie.

"Yup."

"You like it?" To Roxanne.

"Very cool."

"You —"

"Peggy, that's enough." I grabbed her hand. She pulled it back. "Wait, Star. This sweatshirt's too hot. I want my sweater instead."

"Peggy!"

"One minute." She ran back to her room and came back with a sweater our grandma had made her, yellow with blue dinosaurs. "You like my —"

"Forget it. Let's go."

"OK, let me get buttoned up." She started doing up the top button, her chin tucked into her chest so she could see. Of course, being four, her fingers were clumsy and she couldn't get the button through the hole. Impatient glances passed between my friends.

"Here, let me," I said.

"I can do it myself."

Finally she got the sweater buttoned. Then she wiggled. "Too itchy. I'll wear my Kitten Krunchies jacket instead."

More rolled eyes. A few sighs.

"Peg-gy!"

"Don't worry, Star, it's right here." And it was, right on the living room couch, where she'd left it before. Off with the sweater, on with the jacket.

We started for the door. "Maybe my COOL CAT sweat-shirt would be better-"

"Don't even think about it!" I yanked her out the door and dragged her along.

"Star, you're hurting," she complained.

"Tough."

But after a while, I cooled off. We had to go slowly any-way, because of Glynnis, and Miranda took a turn holding Peggy's hand, and then Priya did, so I got a break. By the time we got to the ice cream parlour, I wasn't mad anymore. I was just excited about my salsa ice cream cone.

"The Ice Cream Pagoda!" Julie said. "Great idea, Star."

"You'll love this place," Miranda added.

"I love ice cream anyway," Roxanne said.

"Wait until you see the flavours," Julie told them. "You've never heard of half of them."

We got in line and slowly inched our way to the front. Julie got papaya, Glynnis got pesto, Roxanne got chili, Priya got turnip, Miranda got strawberry ("Chicken!" every-body teased), Frannie got plantain and I got my salsa. It was an alarming shade of orange but really tasty.

"Star," Frannie said, taking a lick of green, "this is the coolest place."

"Aren't you supposed to put this stuff on spaghetti?" Glynnis asked, staring at her light green pesto ice cream.

"I can't believe I'm eating turnips," Priya said. "And loving it."

I grinned. Maybe Peggy had been a pain, but at least the Ice Cream Pagoda was a hit.

We stood around, waiting for my sister to make up her mind.

"Come on, Peggy, what are you going to have?" I said.

"I don't know. I need a taste."

"Which one?"

She pointed to kidney bean. One of the Mr. Hings — the second oldest — gave her a taste on a tiny plastic spoon. "Yummy," she said.

"You want that?"

"I don't know. I need a taste of that one."

She pointed to the watermelon. Mr. Hing gave her a taste.

"That's good."

"You want that?"

"Not sure."

I heard loud sighs behind me.

Next she tasted zucchini.

"Maybe."

"Peggy!"

"I got to be sure, Star."

"Listen, Star," Julie said, touching my arm, "we'll go sit outside, OK?"

"OK," I said. "Sorry, guys. I'll try to move things along. We'll be right out."

Have you ever tried to move along a four-year-old? Forget it.

Boysenberry. Ginger. Curry.

Groaning, I went outside. All my friends were squeezed around a small table. Their heads were bent close together and they were talking in low voices. "Surprise ... " I thought I heard, but it was too soft to be sure. " ... Don't tell ... "

"Don't tell who what?" I joked.

Their heads whipped up. Their voices fell silent. Glances darted around. For a second, I got the feeling there really was something someone wasn't supposed to tell. A secret. About me?

Julie's face was red. "Uh ... what I got you for your birthday. Right, guys?"

"Right, right," they chorused. But it didn't sound convincing. Were they hiding something? No, that was ridiculous. Must be my imagination.

I forced a smile. "Look, guys, I'm really sorry about Peggy, but it shouldn't be too much longer —"

"Actually, Star," Julie said, not quite looking me in the eye, "we're all finished with our cones, so we thought we'd head back."

"To the house?"

"Well, yeah," Frannie said, indicating her empty hands. "Not much point hanging around."

"This way Peggy can take her time, and we don't have to wait," Roxanne pointed out.

"And we can free up a table," Priya said.

"I need a head start, anyway," Glynnis added, pushing herself to her feet and reaching for her crutches.

The others got up, too. I couldn't believe it. They were leaving?

"Thanks for the ice cream, Star," Priya said.

"Yeah, thanks," everyone chimed in, turning away.

*What was going on?*

"You're welcome," I said, trying not to sound like I was mad or hurt or confused at the way they were rushing away, leaving me stranded at my own party. "I'll get back as fast as I can."

I went back inside. Those sure sounded like a bunch of excuses, I thought. *Was* there some kind of secret going on? No, that was impossible. It was just Peggy. Pain-in-the-neck Peggy. They didn't want to wait anymore. And I couldn't blame them. Neither would I.

Peggy was now tasting prune. Then she tried peppermint. Even Mr. Hing, who always says Peggy is the cutest thing that ever lived, looked like he was losing patience.

Chutney. Chicory. Cherry.

I squatted down in front of Peggy, my hands gripping her shoulders. "That's it! I've had it! You're wrecking my party. You're ruining my life. The next flavour you taste, you're getting. You got that? Choose!"

"OK, Star." Peggy smiled sweetly at Mr. Hing. "Vanilla."

It was all I could do to keep my hands off her neck. She got her ice cream and I paid for all the cones. I grabbed her hand.

"Let's go!"

# Chapter Five

As soon as we got home, I dumped Peggy on my parents. Finally! Now my friends and I could get on with the party. I followed the sound of laughter, which seemed to be coming from the living room. I was just rounding the corner from the kitchen when I heard Julie's voice. She was giggling as she spoke. "... knocked a chair over — KABOOM! — crashed to the floor ... made a huge racket ... blew it ... total klutz."

Everyone burst into peals of laughter and I couldn't hear the rest of what Julie said.

I didn't need to. I couldn't believe it.

Julie had told them about the most humiliating experience of my life. My best friend had betrayed me.

I'd better explain. A few months ago, Julie and I both auditioned for a TV production of *The Wizard of Oz*. We were trying out to be Munchkins. For the audition, you had to sing and dance to "Follow the Yellow Brick Road."

Julie was really nervous about the audition. I wasn't. She was freaked out. I figured it was a piece of cake.

Until I got inside the audition room. Then I froze. I stammered. I forgot the words to the song. I squeaked. I tripped over my own feet. And then — while leaping about, supposedly dancing — I knocked over a chair. It fell with a crash. The floor shook. I was a total klutz. It was the most embarrassing moment of my life.

I didn't get the part.

Julie did.

After our auditions, I told her what had happened. She was really nice. She didn't laugh. She didn't rub it in. She never mentioned it again. So naturally, I didn't ask her not to tell anyone about the chair. I didn't think I had to. Because best friends don't tell humiliating things about each other. Julie knew that. She wouldn't tell anyone, ever.

I was wrong. She'd told them. My best friend had gone behind my back and told my deepest secret and laughed at me. At my own birthday party! And this was after I'd worried about helping her fit in. She was fitting in, all right. Gossiping about me and stealing my camp friends right out from under my nose. How could she do that to me?

I was so hurt I could hardly breathe. For what seemed like minutes, I stood in the doorway, listening to the laughter. But I couldn't stay there forever, so finally, trying to look like nothing was wrong, I went into the living room.

At once, the laughter died down. Looks were exchanged. Cheeks turned pink.

If I'd needed proof, that was certainly it.

"Oh, there you are, Star," Julie said in a voice that tried to sound normal but didn't quite make it. "We were wondering when you'd get back."

"Here I am."

"What now, Star?" Priya said in a friendly tone.

"Presents!" Frannie said.

"Yeah, presents!" everyone said, and ran to get their gifts.

What presents. A beach towel with a picture of a black widow spider on it from Miranda. A book called *Groaners: The World's Worst Riddles and Jokes* from Glynnis. A sweatshirt that said I'M AN ARACHNOPHILE — AND PROUD OF IT in fuzzy letters, from Frannie and Priya. A poster titled "Everything You Ever Wanted to Know About Elvis ... But Were Afraid to Ask," with about four-hundred facts about Elvis's life, from Roxanne.

Finally, Julie's. Small but heavy. When I tore off the paper, I saw that the box was from the Science Shoppe. My heart started pounding. I'd dragged Julie in there a few weeks ago and showed her ...

Yes, she'd got it. The magnifying glass. The one with the wooden handle and the glass bound in shiny steel. The one with the extra little magnifier, for looking at tiny specimens, that was tucked inside the handle and sprang out when you pushed a button, and then tucked back in again like a hidden trap door.

I was totally confused. How could she make fun of me and then give me the thing I wanted most? How could she be so rotten and then so great?

Maybe, I thought, I'd been mistaken. Maybe Julie hadn't

told them. Maybe I'd imagined the whole thing.

"Thanks, guys," I said, and meant it. I gave Julie a special smile and she smiled back.

Yeah, I thought, I must have misunderstood. Julie was too good a friend to do that.

"Now what, Star?" Miranda said.

"We could look up Elvis facts," Roxanne suggested.

"Roxanne," Frannie protested, giving her a shove.

Roxanne toppled over, giggling, then bounced back up. "I could sing more Elvis songs."

Frannie gave her another shove.

Roxanne popped up again. "I could recite Elvis's lines in *Love Me Tender*. It was his very first movie, you know."

"Speaking of movies, Julie, weren't you just in *The Wizard of Oz*?" Glynnis said. I froze. *The Wizard of Oz*? Was this supposed to be some kind of coincidence? No way! Julie must have told them. Why else would Glynnis have brought up *The Wizard of Oz*?

So I hadn't been mistaken after all. The rat!

Julie blushed. "Yeah."

"Would you do your part for us?"

"Me? Here?"

"Sure, why not? Star always told us what a great actress you were."

"Oh, I don't know," Julie said, blushing.

"Come on," Glynnis said. "We'd really like to see it, wouldn't we, guys?"

"Yeah, come on, Julie," they all chimed in.

Julie gave a modest little cough — she was a great actress, all right. "I'm sure there's something else you'd rather do."

"No, we want you," Roxanne said, and they all took up the chant, "We want the Munchkin! We want the Munchkin!"

Shooting me an apologetic look — yeah, I bet she was so sorry about rubbing it in — Julie stood up. "Well, if you insist."

She pointed her foot, holding out her make-believe skirt. "Follow the yellow brick road, follow the yellow brick road … " She did the dance steps perfectly. She sang on key. She whirled gracefully. She smiled at her adoring audience. Soon they were clapping and singing along, "We're off to the see the Wizard, the wonderful Wizard of Oz." (That was where, in the audition, I'd knocked over the chair.) "We hear he is a whiz of a wiz, if ever a wiz there was …" (That was where I'd crossed my feet up.) "The wonderful Wizard of Oz!" (That was where I'd finished with my back to the judges. Where I'd blown it once and for all.)

Julie finished with a twirl and a curtsey. Ecstatic applause erupted. Roxanne wolf-whistled.

"That was great!"

"Wow!"

"You really are good!"

Flushed, grinning, Julie sat down.

Some friends. Some birthday. Some party.

"So, Star, what's next?" Miranda said.

Too miserable to say anything, I just shrugged. Roxanne pulled a videotape out of her backpack — Elvis Presley in *Viva Las Vegas* — and we ended up watching that.

I couldn't tell you what it was about. I didn't see a thing.

One by one, my friends drifted off to sleep. I was the last one awake. I lay there

in my sleeping bag, listening to the quiet breathing of my so-called friends, thinking what a rotten birthday party this was.

Then I realized something even more rotten. I had completely forgotten to tell them about the fanged vampire spider. Forgotten to ask for their help. Now it was too late. Besides, who would want to help me, knowing what a klutz and a loser I was? And I didn't want their lousy help anyway. Any of them, even Julie. Especially Julie.

So now I was on my own. I'd have to collect three thousand signatures all by myself.

Which was impossible. The whole thing was doomed.

# Chapter Six

We were at my grandma's for three weeks. When I got home, there was a letter from Camp Crescent Moon and three postcards from Julie. (She was in Hong Kong, visiting relatives. Her family always spends July there.)

The letter from camp said:

Dear Star,
WE MISS YOU!! Not the same without you. Joey and Todd are still going strong, boomba-boomba! No good pranks without you. Ruth can't believe how good we are. Though I (Glynnis) did manage to hide all the oatmeal in the broom closet so we couldn't have gross porridge for breakfast, but the cook found it. Fooey. Wish you were here! See you soon!!

It was signed by Glynnis, Roxanne, Priya, Frannie and Miranda.

Julie's postcards said:

Hi, Star,
How's it going? Hot and humid here. My brothers are a pain in the neck. How's your grandma? Write me.
Love, Julie

Hey, Star,
Did you get my postcard? Write, OK? I long to hear your goofy voice. I have a new baby cousin who can almost shove her whole fist in her mouth. Miss you.
Jule

Star —
Write me already, will you? Two more weeks and then I'll be home and we can go to the beach and go rollerblading and play Checkers (I'm getting better, I'm warning you) and hang out. Can't wait to see you.
Your best friend, Julie

*Yeah, right!* My best friend. Acting as if nothing happened. All of them, acting as if they were my good friends and they'd never laughed at me and told secrets about me. What did they think I was, stupid? That I'd forgive and forget?

They had another think coming.

Especially Julie.

I didn't write back.

But now I had to face a problem. A big problem. How on earth was I going to collect 3,000 signatures for the *Araneus vampiricus*?

I did some math. If I could get ten signatures a day — and that was probably a lot — it would take me ... let's see ... 10 into 3,000 ... 10 into 30 is 3, plus a zero, plus another zero ... 300. Three hundred days! That was nearly a year. A year of pounding the streets and knocking on doors. Think of all the pencils I'd go through. Think of all the shoes I'd wear out. Think of the blisters.

Then a horrible thought occurred to me. What if someone else came along during that year, someone with a different spider, someone with lots of friends to help, and got three thousand signatures before I did? Then some other spider would be the Provincial Arachnid.

No! I couldn't let that happen.

Maybe, I thought, I should ask Julie and the others anyway. Swallow my pride and beg. After all, what was more important, my hurt feelings or getting the fanged vampire spider named the Provincial Arachnid? That was a tough one, but in the end I decided the spider was. My province needed a Provincial Arachnid. When my friends got home, I decided, I'd try to forget what had happened and ask for their help.

About a week later, I ran into Julie at the library. Literally. She was running in and I was running out and we collided. In the first moment, I was so happy to see her, I forgot everything and said, "Jule! When did you get back?"

She glared at me. "Thanks a lot for not writing."

She was mad? What was *she* mad about? After writing those fake, everything-is-normal postcards? "Yeah, as if you meant what you said."

"Huh?"

"'Miss you.' 'Can't wait to see you.' Sure, Jule."

She looked shocked. "What?"

"Oh, come on, I know phony when I see it."

Her cheeks turned crimson. "Are you calling me phony?"

People passing us on the library steps were staring, but I didn't care. "Yeah! You're not that good of an actress, even if you were in the *Wizard of Oz*."

"The *Wizard of Oz*? What's that got to do with it?"

"Oh, yeah, pretend you don't know."

She put her hands on her hips. "Star, what is going on? Ever since your party, you've been really weird."

"Well, I wonder why," I said sarcastically.

She stared at me. "So do I," she said, and pushed past me into the library.

Boy, I was steamed. First she'd betrayed me and then she had the nerve to get mad at me for not writing cheerful little letters.

Well, forget asking her for help.

I stormed away, arms swinging, feet pounding, not caring where I walked. After a few blocks, I found myself at the Ice Cream Pagoda. The usual summertime crowd spilled out the door. I felt in my pocket. I still had some money from my allowance. An ice cream cone wouldn't be a bad idea right now, so I got in line. Slowly I inched forward, up the sidewalk, onto the steps, in the door. Boy, the place was jammed. Behind the counter, all the Hings were piling ice cream into cones as fast as they could.

I looked around to see if there was anyplace to sit, and I saw them. Miranda, Priya, Frannie and Roxanne, crowded around one of the tiny tables, eating ice cream cones, hunched over some papers spread out on the table.

"Hey, you guys," I called.

Miranda's head came up. She looked surprised. Her face turned red. "Star," she choked.

The others turned. "Star," they chorused, as if I were the last person they expected to see. Quickly they gathered up the papers and Roxanne slid them onto her lap.

"Fancy meeting you here," Priya said with a nervous chuckle.

"Hey, how you doing?" Frannie said in an almost-normal voice. "When'd you get back?"

I went over to the table. What was going on? What were the papers? Those guys were up to something, that was for sure. And I wasn't part of it, that was for sure, too.

Cripes, what was it about the Ice Cream Pagoda? Every

time I went there, somebody was keeping secrets from me.

"Did you get our letter?" Roxanne said. She leaned over as if she was scratching her foot, but I saw her stuff the papers into a backpack on the floor.

"Yeah, I got it. How's it going, you guys?"

"Fine, fine," Priya said, darting glances at the others.

"Look, Star, I got garlic this time," Frannie said, holding out a creamy white ice cream cone. "Pretty brave, huh?"

"Then she's going to kiss everybody," Miranda said, and they all laughed. A little too loudly.

"Hilarious, guys," I said. "I don't suppose anyone would like to tell me what's going on?"

Silence.

"What?" Miranda said innocently.

"Nothing," Frannie added.

"Yeah, right."

"Really, Star," Roxanne said. "We're just enjoying a little ice cream on a hot day. Why don't you get some and join us?"

They squished their chairs together, making room. "Yeah, join us, Star."

I looked from one to the other, around the circle. "No, thanks. I'm not hungry anymore."

I left.

Forget about asking them, too, I told myself. I definitely wasn't imagining anything this time. They were up to something and they didn't want me to know about it.

Well, they could keep their secrets. And Julie could keep pretending that she hadn't done anything wrong. I'd been ready to beg, but I wasn't going to beg now. There was only one person I could count on to get the signatures, and that was me. And I'd better get going.

# Chapter Seven

I went home, got a clipboard and pad, and wrote at the top, YES! I WANT THE ARANEUS VAMPIRICUS TO BE THE OFFICAL PROVINCIAL ARACHNID OF BRITISH COLUMBIA! Then I grabbed a picture of the spider and ran over to Mrs. Wentworth's house. She's our next door neighbour.

"Oh, hello, Starshine," she said, opening the door.

"Hi, Mrs. Wentworth. I was wondering —"

Hughie bounded up. Hughie is Mrs. Wentworth's black lab. Hughie loves me. I love him, too. I play with him all the time. Only right now wasn't a very good time.

When Hughie saw it was me, he started wagging his tail. Whack-whack-whack went his tail against the door.

"Yes, honey? You were wondering —"

"Yeah, I was wondering if you'd like to sign —"

Hughie pushed his nose against me, hard. "Hi, Hughie, that's a good boy," I said, scratching him between the ears, the way he likes. Whack-whack-whack-whack-whack went his tail, twice as fast. Then he took off.

"Would you like to sign —"

Back came Hughie with his ball. He dropped it at my feet with a plop. A wet plop.

Hughie is a great dog, but he's also a slobbery dog. His ball is an old, bald tennis ball that's so full of slobber, it would sink if you dropped it in water. It's slimy and squishy and it smells like old dog's breath.

Whack-whack-whack-whack-whack. Nudge-nudge.

I picked up Hughie's ball and heaved it to the far end of Mrs. Wentworth's lawn, hoping that would give me enough time to explain —

"Is that schoolwork you've got there, Starshine?" she said, peering at my clipboard. "In the summertime? I declare, they work children so hard these days, they don't even have a chance to be children."

"No, Mrs. Wentworth, it's not schoolwork, it's a —"

"Poor little kids, running from activity to activity, learning to read before they're even out of diapers. It's a crime, that's all, and I'd like to give their parents a piece of my mind —"

"Actually, Mrs. Wentworth, it has nothing to do with school —"

"What happened to good old-fashioned play, I ask you? Frolicking about, playing pretend games? No time anymore. No, they march these little tykes like soldiers —"

Plop. Hughie was back, his tongue hanging out, looking at me adoringly. I threw the ball.

"— from piano lessons to soccer, from soccer to choir, from choir to basketball. And extra schoolwork thrown in on top of that —"

I didn't know what to do. I'd never seen Mrs. Wentworth so worked up. Her face was red and her finger stabbed the air.

In desperation, I waved the picture of the *Araneus vampiricus* at her.

"— just to make sure they get straight A's — What's that?"

"It's a spider, Mrs. Wentworth. *Araneus vampiricus*. The fanged vampire spider. I'm trying to have it named the Provincial Arachnid of British Columbia."

Mrs. Wentworth looked from the picture to my clipboard. "Not homework?"

"No."

"Nothing to do with school?"

"No."

"Nor extracurricular activities?"

"No."

"Well, bless my soul, why didn't you say so in the first place?"

After I explained about the petition, Mrs. Wentworth shook her head. "It's a worthy cause, Starshine, and I'm happy to support it. But 3,000 signatures? How on earth will you manage that?"

I managed a smile. "I haven't got the faintest idea, Mrs. Wentworth. But I'm going to try."

"Well, good for you." She signed her name with a flourish: Mrs. Olive Alexandra (Richardson) Wentworth. It spilled over onto the second line. Maybe it would count for two. "There you go, Starshine. And good luck."

"Thanks. I'll need it."

Plop.

"Sorry, Hughie, got to go." He gazed at me imploringly. "Oh, all right, one more time."

The Hoopers lived next door to Mrs. Wentworth. They were a young couple. They jogged and rode bikes and were into nature. I was sure they'd sign.

Mrs. Hooper came to the door. She was pregnant. Very pregnant. Her stomach practically pushed me off the doorstep.

"Oh, hello, Starshine. What's up?" She put one hand in the small of her back and leaned against the doorframe.

"Hi, Mrs. Hooper. You — uh — feeling OK?"

She smiled, shaking her head. "Queasy. Very queasy. It's amazing this squirt is growing the way it is, considering I can hardly keep anything down. Thank God for ginger ale."

"Ginger ale?"

"Yeah, it's good for settling an upset stomach. I bet I've drunk a bathtub full of the stuff already." She laughed. "Anyway, what can I do for you?"

I explained.

"A spider?" She began to turn pale.

"Yeah, it's called the fanged vampire spider and it eats slugs."

"Slugs?" From pale to yellow.

"Yeah. Here's what it looks like." I held up the picture. "It's really a pretty spider, with those red and yellow stripes. See?"

From yellow to green. She started backing up. "Sorry, Starshine, I don't think I can —" She gulped. "Oh dear, I think I —" She clamped her hand over her mouth. "Excuse me —"

She ran, or, rather, waddled away.

So much for the Hoopers.

An older man lived in the next house. I didn't know him very well. No one did. He was the kind of person who kept his light turned off on Halloween, so he wouldn't have to give out any candy.

I didn't want to go to his house, but I was desperate.

He came to the door, holding a newspaper. "Yes, what is it?" he said impatiently, glaring at me over his glasses.

"Well, yes, hello, my name is Starshine Shapiro, I live down the street, just two doors away. Well, three, actually, if you count yours, and I —"

He looked at my clipboard. "If this is a spell-a-thon or a math-a-thon, or whatever they call those danged things, forget it. I'm not interested."

"No, no, it's not a spell-a-thon —"

"Oh, I get it. You're taking donations, right? Collecting for some cause? Should have known. Well, I don't donate. To anybody or anything."

He went to shut the door.

"No, it's nothing like that," I said.

He stopped, his hand on the door. "Well, then? Get to the point."

I would if you'd let me, you old grouch, I thought, but I smiled sweetly and explained about the petition. He actually listened, until I said, "...and if I get enough signatures, the provincial government will proclaim the *Araneus vampiricus* the Provincial Arachnid —"

"Provincial government!" he shouted. "I'll tell you about the provincial government! Those jokers. All they want to do is raise taxes and spend, spend, spend. Jetting around at taxpayers' expense. And do they do anything useful? Not on your life. The crooks! The scoundrels! The —"

I left him there, ranting.

Things were looking grim. I'd been out for over an hour and had only one signature.

But the next house was a pretty sure bet. A sweet old lady, Mrs. Chalmers, lived there. She was forever baking cookies and giving them to me and Peggy when we went by.

I rang the bell.

"Oh, hello, there," she said, wiping her hands on her apron. A delicious smell floated out the door. "Samantha, is it?"

"Starshine."

"Oh yes, of course, Starshine. You'd think I'd remember an unusual name like that, wouldn't you? Just shows how forgetful I'm getting. Well, come in, come in, Susannah. Would you like an oatmeal cookie? Fresh out of the oven."

She led me into the kitchen. Trays of cookies were cooling on the counters, on the table, on the stovetop. Everywhere, in fact, except on a buffet at one end of the kitchen, the kind of thing that people display fancy dishes in, with glassed-in shelves — and the only reason there weren't cookies cooling on *it* was because there wasn't room; little knick-knacks covered the top of it.

"Sure, Mrs. Chalmers, thanks."

She put about a dozen cookies on a plate. "Milk? Can't have cookies without milk."

"Well … sure. Thanks."

While I ate cookies and drank milk, Mrs. Chalmers told me that her  grandchildren loved her oatmeal cookies; they loved all her cookies, of course, but oatmeal the best, and the next thing I knew, I was looking at pictures of four little kids and hearing how smart the oldest was, like a whip, and what a good athlete his sister was, the fastest runner on her T-ball team, and how the twins, the two littlest ones, were always wearing each other's clothes and fooling everybody, the scamps.

I kept trying to bring up the petition, but every time I opened my mouth, Mrs. Chalmers launched into a new subject, so I kept eating more cookies and drinking more milk. My stomach began to hurt.

Now she was telling me about a trip she'd made to Victoria last week.

I swallowed in a hurry. "It's funny you should mention Victoria, Mrs. Chalmers," I said, talking fast, "because that's what I came to talk to you about. Sort of. See, my class went to Victoria, to the Royal British Columbia Museum, and I noticed that there was no Provincial Arachnid. There are all kinds of other Provincial Symbols, but no —"

"Provincial Symbols?" Mrs. Chalmers interrupted. "Did you say Provincial Symbols?"

For a minute I thought she was going to start ranting about the government, like the guy next door, but then she put her hand on her heart. "I love our Provincial Symbols, and our Provincial Flower, dogwood, most of all, Sarah."

"Starshine."

"Oh yes, Starshine." She pulled me up from my chair. "Come over here and see my dogwood collection."

Before I knew it, she'd dragged me across the kitchen, over to the buffet with the glass doors. And now, as I looked closely, I saw that all the doodads were dogwood stuff. China statues of dogwood trees, the tiny leaves and flowers painted with dots of green and white ... dogwood-engraved silver spoons ... silk dogwood flowers in a branch-shaped vase ... a deck of dogwood playing cards ... a crocheted tea cosy with dogwood flowers ... a dogwood-shaped ashtray ... a pillow with dogwood flowers embroidered all over it ... dogwood salt and pepper shakers. It was a shrine to dogwood.

"This is ... uh ... well, it's incredible, Mrs. Chalmers," I said.

"It's the largest collection of dogwood memorabilia in British Columbia."

"I can believe it."

"Possibly in the world."

"I can believe that, too."

"I've been collecting for forty-seven years."

"Wow. Whatever possessed you — I mean, what made you start collecting dogwood?"

She flapped her hand. "Why, what a ridiculous question! It's our Provincial Flower, isn't it? Do I love this province or don't I?"

I wasn't sure if she was actually asking me, but I answered, "You love it, Mrs. Chalmers."

"You're darn right I do! Don't you?"

"Well, yeah, sure I do."

"Of course you do! We both do." Mrs. Chalmers put her arm around me and I thought she was going to burst into song. "We love our province. And we love our Provincial Symbols. Our Dogwood. Our Steller's Jay. Our Jade. Our —"

Inspiration hit me. Turning to face her, I put both hands on her shoulders. "I'm with you, Mrs. Chalmers. Crazy about those Provincial Symbols, that's us. And Mrs. Chalmers, what would you say if I told you that you could *add* to the list of Provincial Symbols, so there would be even more of them?"

"More Provincial Symbols? Oh, my. What do I have to do? Tell me, tell me!"

I whipped out the clipboard. "Sign here."

Her face glowing, she signed.

"Good work, Mrs. Chalmers. That's the B.C. spirit."

She wiped the corner of her eye with her apron. "Just think. I, Doris Chalmers, have helped to make British Columbia a better place." She sighed happily. "Now, here, take a few more cookies with you, Sandra." She stuffed half a dozen cookies into my pocket. "And come back soon. Next time, I'll show you my dogwood postcards. All two hundred of them."

I escaped.

Well, that did it for our block. I had two signatures — and a stomachache.

Burp.

Oh, dear. I really had eaten too many cookies.

I remembered what Mrs. Hooper had said about ginger ale. I still had that money — I'd never bought the ice cream cone — so I figured I'd go to the corner store, get a can of ginger ale and then tackle the other side of the street. Maybe I could double my total and get four big ones.

While I was drinking the ginger ale, sip by burpy sip, I looked at the bulletin board outside the corner store. It was full of notices: cars for sale, apartments for rent, lost cats, garage sales. Then I noticed another poster. At the top there was a picture of a slug, a cartoon-style slug, with a big smile on its face. Beneath that, it said:

---

## SOCIETY FOR THE PRESERVATION OF SLUGS

SLUG-SUPPORTERS UNITE!
DON'T LET DO-GOODERS
DESTROY THE NOBLE SLUG!
PROTECT SLUGS FOREVER!

JOIN THE SOCIETY FOR THE
PRESERVATION OF SLUGS!
SHOW SLUG SOLIDARITY!

CALL ROB O'SHEA, PRESIDENT

---

*Society for the Preservation of Slugs!*
*No-o-o-o!*

This was the worst, the absolute worst. A group dedicated to saving slugs! Naturally, they would hate the fanged vampire spider. The fanged vampire spider would be their enemy. And as for having it named the Provincial Arachnid, they'd never let that happen. In fact, they'd probably want all fanged vampire spiders destroyed.

And they had posters. They had a society with a phone number and address. They were organized. Against this kind of opposition, I didn't have a chance.

It looked like my *Araneus vampiricus* project was dead in its tracks. Squashed flatter than a dead spider.

# Chapter Eight

When I got home, Peggy had a friend over.

I was in no mood for Peggy – or anyone else. For one thing, I was still mad at her for wrecking my birthday party. For another thing, I was bummed out about the Society for the Preservation of Slugs. For a third thing, my stomach was killing me.

Peggy and her friend were sprawled on the living room floor in front of a gigantic Lego castle.

Peggy jumped up. "Star, look who's here," she chirped, "Kirsten!"

So this was the wondrous Kirsten — Peggy's new best friend from preschool. For weeks I'd been hearing about this kid. Peggy worshipped her. She had to wear her hair in pigtails, like Kirsten, even though her hair wasn't long enough and she ended up with two stubby pigtails sticking out from the sides of her head. And she had to have peanut butter sandwiches for a snack, like Kirsten, even though she hated peanut butter. And she had to bring her juice in a pink thermos because Kirsten had a pink thermos.

It was really weird. Peggy wasn't the type to go ga-ga over another kid. In fact, she's usually the popular one, the one other kids flock to. But she'd sure gone ga-ga over Kirsten.

Right now, I didn't feel like meeting anyone, let alone some four-year-old preschooler. But in spite of myself, I was curious about Kirsten. What could possibly be so great about her?

"Hi, Kirsten," I said.

She glanced up. Well, she was cute, that was for sure. Head full of golden-blonde curls, freckled upturned nose, huge green eyes, chubby cheeks.

"Hi," she said without any interest, then turned back to Peggy, hand outstretched. "Give me the tower, Peggy."

Whoa. A little lacking in manners here? A little bossy?

Peggy placed a red piece of Lego in her hand. Carefully Kirsten pressed it on top of the castle. "There. I finished it. Look what a good job I did."

"You did great, Kirsten. It's the best castle I ever saw," Peggy said, gazing at her like a puppy gazing at its master.

*What?* This really was weird, the way Peggy was fawning all over her. It sure wasn't like my bossy sister.

Oh, well, I thought, flopping down on the couch, it wasn't my problem. I had enough of my own. Like no friends. Like three thousand signatures. Like the Society for the Preservation of Slugs.

With a sigh, I propped the clipboard on my lap and started making copies of the petition. I didn't know why I was bothering. My spider campaign probably didn't have a chance. But at the moment it was the only thing I could think of to do.

Meanwhile, Peggy was gazing at Kirsten, while Kirsten was admiring her castle. "What do you want to do now, Kirsten?" Peggy said.?

"Paint," Kirsten replied.

Peggy hesitated. I didn't blame her. The paints were in our mom and dad's studio. Our dad was out, installing the stained glass window in the rich people's house, and our mom was in the studio, working. Even at four and a half, Peggy knows that when our mom is in her "creative space," especially when she's "giving birth" to a new pot, it is definitely not good to interrupt. When you live with artists, you learn these things fast. Especially when you've had your head bitten off a few times.

"I can't bother my mom when she's working," Peggy said.

Attagirl, I thought, surprised to find myself rooting for her.

"I want to paint." More forcefully.

Peggy hesitated. I could tell she didn't want to go in there.

"I guess I can just go home," Kirsten said quietly.

A look of alarm crossed Peggy's face. "No, don't, Kirsten. I'll get the paints." She trudged off to the studio.

I couldn't believe it. What was going on with Peggy? Why was she letting Kirsten do this to her?

Not that I cared, I thought as I started a new page. Peggy was a pain. A spoiled, showoffy, slowpoke pain. But for some strange reason, it bothered me to see her get treated like that.

Sure enough, I heard my mom scold her when she barged into the studio. Peggy came out a minute later, looking sheepish, dragging the easels. Then she went back for the paints and the water jars and the brushes and the smocks. She set every-thing up in the kitchen. She got each of them a jar of water and gave Kirsten first pick of the brushes.

Kirsten chose the biggest and best paintbrush, dipped it in the red paint and made a few strokes on the paper. She just kind of slapped it on, as if she didn't really care what she was doing.

Meanwhile, Peggy was really getting into her picture. She loves art. She actually inherited some of our parents' talent. (Good thing one of us did.) She made a purple squiggle and a yellow blob and a green zigzag, carefully cleaning her brush between each colour, and stepping back to consider what to do next, and was just feathering in some orange strokes when Kirsten put her brush down, without cleaning it, and said, "I'm bored of this. Let's do something else."

Peggy stopped, paintbrush in the air. "Something else?"

Kirsten rolled her eyes. "Peg-gy, come on."

Surely, I thought, Peggy would let her have it this time. After she went to all that trouble. But she just put down her brush. "What do you want to do now, Kirsten?"

*What?*

"Well … " Kirsten said … "how's about we play dress-up?"

"OK!" Peggy said. "I'll get the dress-up clothes." She dragged the big dress-up box into the living room, and she and Kirsten started tossing out clothes. Lacy slips and elbow-length gloves … a black pirate patch … clunky "high heels" … a magic wand … cloaks and capes … old lady hats with cloth roses on the brim …

Kirsten pulled out a frilly crinoline. "Oh, I like this!" she said. "It's like a fancy ball gown. Like a queen wears. I'll be the queen."

"OK," Peggy said, "I'll be the princess."

Kirsten shook her head. "Unh-unh. You have to be the prince."

Peggy looked stunned. "W-why?"

"'Cause there's only one girl in this game, and I'm it, so you have to be a boy."

Peggy looked dismayed. But only for a moment. She grabbed the magic wand. My dad had made it. The wand part was a thin bar of the kind of metal he uses in his stained glass windows, and he'd fastened a multi-coloured glass star to the end. "I know! I'll be a fairy. Not a girl or a boy. Just a magic fairy."

Kirsten grabbed the wand out of her hand. "No, I need this. 'Cause I'm a queen-magic fairy. I have to have it."

I was waiting for Peggy to sock her, but she just stood there looking miserable. I couldn't believe it. My sister Peggy — the brat — the mouth — was taking this?

Kirsten pulled a brown shirt from the box.

"Here, Prince, this is your cape. Put it on."

Glumly, Peggy put it on.

"Now," Kirsten said, throwing a silver scarf around her shoulders for a royal robe, "you're a bad prince —"

"No! I don't want to be a bad prince. I'm good!"

Kirsten's curls bounced as she shook her head. "Nuh-uh. You're bad 'cause you put a spell on the royal princess and turned her into a pig. But I, the Queen-Magic Fairy, am going to wave my magic wand — ka-pow! — and undo your wicked spell. And now I'm going to punish you. Bad Prince, you must scrub all the floors in the palace! Now, get to work!" She pointed a commanding finger.

Peggy fell to her knees. "Yes, Your Majesty," she said, scrubbing away with an imaginary cloth, "I won't make any more bad spells and then I'll be a good prince."

"We'll see," Kirsten said.

Just then there was a knock at the door. I opened it. A beautiful blonde woman was standing there. "Hello, there," she said with a glamourous smile, "is Kirsten here?"

"Mommy!" Kirsten cried. She tossed down the wand, tore off the cape and the crinoline and threw them on the floor. "'Bye, Peggy."

Peggy jumped up. "'Bye, Kirsten. Play with me tomorrow?"

"Maybe."

The little brat! I thought, watching her curls bounce out the door.

And then I remembered. I knew why it had bothered me so much to see Peggy treated that way. Because the same thing had happened to me. Only my "Kirsten" was named Patti Nyberg.

Patti was the prettiest and the smartest and the most popular kid in my grade one class. Everybody followed her. Everybody wanted to be like her. Everybody competed to be her best friend. To be chosen by Patti, even just to play with at recess, was to be special.

And for some mysterious and wonderful reason, Patti Nyberg chose me. We strolled the playground at recess, arm in arm. We shared snacks: she always had gooey cupcakes, while all I had was bricks, my dad's health food cookies. But miraculously she didn't mind and I ate her cupcakes and got stomachaches.

"You're my best friend, Patti," I'd say.

"Mmm-hmm," she'd reply.

We gossiped about the other kids. Well, Patti gossiped and I ate it up, because if she said bad things about other people, that meant she liked me better, right?

"Miranda Stockton's underpants are showing," she said one time, and I snickered. I didn't have anything against Miranda, but if being Patti's best friend meant laughing at other kids, I'd laugh.

"Miranda cuts pictures crooked," she added.

"Stupid-head," I replied.

One time she said, "Miranda wets her bed." Oh, that was a good one, and I told Lucy Chatham and Lucy told Miranda and Miranda cried and I secretly felt ashamed because I knew it was mean and it might not even be true. But Patti Nyberg liked me best.

Then one day I came to school and she was arm in arm with Miranda. She shared her snack with Miranda. She played hopscotch with Miranda.

I said, "But, Patti, you promised to play with me! We're best friends." She turned and looked at me — I can see her face so clearly — and the look went right through me, as if I wasn't there, and she turned back to Miranda and they started giggling. "Starshine has poopy snacks," I heard her whisper.

Luckily, Patti Nyberg moved away that year.

But I can still remember how it felt when she dropped me. Boy, did it hurt. And I had a sinking feeling that was exactly how Peggy was going to feel when Kirsten dumped her. And she would. The Kirstens and Pattis of the world always do.

Poor Peggy. Even though I couldn't stand her half the time, I couldn't help feeling sorry for her. I wanted to tell her to forget Kirsten and find a new friend, a real friend.

But then, who was I to give advice about friends? I'd thought I had true-blue friends, and look how wrong I'd been. My supposed best friend had made fun of me behind my back, and my other friends had gone along with the joke. In fact, at the moment I didn't have any friends. Some expert I was.

At dinner that night Peggy seemed to have forgotten all about Kirsten's shenanigans. "Kirsten was here today, Daddy, and we had so much fun!" she gushed.

"Did you, Pumpkin? What did you do?"

"Well, we built a Lego castle and Kirsten put the very top tower on, and we played dress-up and Kirsten was the queen-magic fairy, and we painted —"

"You painted! Can I see your picture?"

For a moment her eyes shifted. "Well … it's not finished,

Daddy." Her face lit up again. "And Kirsten said I'm her best friend, and she doesn't like Gillian anymore, 'cause Gillian is a poo-poo."

"Peggy, that's enough of that," my mom scolded.

Peggy chattered away. Meanwhile, I was pushing my lentil loaf around my plate. Ordinarily, I love lentil loaf, but my stomach was still a bit upset from all the oatmeal cookies. (The ginger ale hadn't helped, either; maybe you had to be pregnant.)

And besides, how could I think about food? I had a bigger problem: the Society for the Preservation of Slugs. I'd copied out half a dozen petitions, but what good were they going to do me with those slug-lovers out there, ruining everything? But what could I do, me against a whole society? There might be hundreds of members, thousands even, in Vancouver, British Columbia, Canada, the world! And all those thousands would know other people. Right now, at this very moment, while I was sitting helplessly at my dinner table, each of them might be out persuading their friends to save slugs.

It seemed hopeless. But I couldn't give up — not without a fight.

But where to start?

Then I remembered I'd copied down the name and address of the President of the Society. I snuck a look at the paper, which was in my pocket, sticky with oatmeal cookie crumbs. Rob O'Shea, his name was. And the address was only a few blocks away. I hadn't noticed that earlier, in my panic.

Well, tomorrow I'd start with him. What other choice did I have? Somehow I had to convince him to lay off — 'cause if he had his way, everybody would want to save slugs and nobody would sign my petition. And that would be the end of my dream to make the fanged vampire spider British Columbia's Provincial Arachnid.

# Chapter Nine

*Please, Mr. O'Shea, I beg you to stop protecting slugs,* I rehearsed as I walked down the street.

*I'm telling you, Mr. O'Shea, you must disband the Society for the Preservation of Slugs.*

*Geez, Mr. O'Shea, who in their right mind likes slugs anyway?*

I turned the corner, and there it was. A nice little stucco house with pink roses in the front — and a slug-loving monster inside.

I rang the bell. A kid answered. A boy, a little older than me, twelve, thirteen maybe, with carrot-red hair, and freckles covering practically every inch of his skin. He slouched against the doorframe, hands in his pockets. Pinned to his T-shirt was a button with a picture of a slug on it.

So the dad has brainwashed the son, I thought. Bad sign.

"Yes?" Friendly smile. I didn't trust it.

"Is Mr. O'Shea home?"

"No, he's at work." He looked at me oddly, as if wondering why I was asking for his dad.

Shoot! I thought. Of course he'd be at work. I should have thought of that. Now I'd come for nothing.

"Can I help you?" the boy said.

"No, never mind."

"Who is it, Rob?" a woman's voice called from the back of the house.

*Rob?*

"Some girl, Mom," he yelled.

"Are you Rob O'Shea?" I asked.

"Yeah." He looked surprised that I knew his name.

"*The* Rob O'Shea? The President of the Society for the Preservation of Slugs?"

A slow smile spread across his face. "You saw my poster? Cool!"

My head was spinning. It had never occurred to me that the President of the Society for the Preservation of Slugs might be a kid. Maybe I had a chance. After all, we were both kids. That made us more or less equal. And he didn't look particularly tough. In fact, the way he was leaning lazily against the door, he looked pretty easy-going. Maybe I could get him to back off.

Sure I could.

I put on my most determined look. "Yes, I saw your poster. And I'm telling you, Rob O'Shea, you've got to stop this business about saving slugs."

He looked surprised. I thought he might agree and that would be the end of it. But he shook his head and quietly said, "Nope."

"But you've got to," I said urgently. "It's really important!"

He slouched deeper into the doorway. "No, no, you've got it wrong. The important thing is to just let slugs be. Just leave 'em alone. Slugs have rights too, you know."

"Rights?" I said, outraged. "What rights? Slugs are worthless blobs —"

He smiled. "That's why they're so great — 'cause they're worthless blobs."

I was beginning to panic. This guy might look easy-going but he was no pushover. "Slugs don't do anything useful. They just sit there like big lumps."

He nodded slowly, as if I'd finally got it. "Right. That's why they should be preserved." Big sigh. "But everywhere you turn, do-gooders are running around, accomplishing things. Tearing down the good name of the slug."

I was on the verge of tears. This guy wouldn't budge. And it seemed the more riled up I got, the more laid-back he got. "Good name?" I shrieked. "What good name? Everybody hates slugs!"

A pained expression crossed his face as he slid lower in the doorway. The guy was practically sitting. "I know, it's totally unfair. Nobody gives a slug an even break." He raised his hands, palms up. "I mean, I didn't want to start the Society, I was forced to — to convince the world to stop hassling slugs and just leave them in peace."

*Convince the world?* Oh, no! "But they're slimy and squishy and eat everything in sight —"

"Just give 'em a chance to veg out once in a while. But no,

everybody's always after you to do your homework or mow the lawn or —"

He stopped.

I stopped.

We stared at each other.

"You mean —" we both said at once, "— the slug —"

"— as in … a lazy person?" I finished.

"— as in … the real thing?" he said.

He smiled.

I smiled.

"I thought … "

"I thought … "

"You mean, people who just lay around?" I said, grinning. "Couch potatoes?"

"You mean, the animal?" he said, grinning back. "The insect?"

"Mollusc!" I said, laughing. "Slugs are molluscs!" And without thinking, I threw my arms around him and gave him a great big hug. Then I realized what I was doing and dropped my arms. My face burned. "Sorry!"

"Hey, I don't mind," he said with a grin. But his cheeks were pink, too.

"I don't usually go around hugging strange guys," I explained, embarrassed.

"You don't?"

"No!" Then I realized he was teasing and we both laughed. "I was just so glad you didn't mean real slugs."

"Those disgusting things? Why would I want to save *them*?"

"That's what I was wondering," I said. "But then, why'd you put up that poster?"

Grinning, he darted a look over his shoulder, making sure his mom didn't hear, I guessed. "It was just a joke. My mom was forever nagging me. You know, 'All you ever do is sit in front of the TV like a slug; why aren't you doing your homework, you're such a slug; why aren't you cleaning your room, blah blah blah.' So I formed the Society for the Preservation of Slugs. As a protest. To defend my right to do nothing. To veg out. To be a lazy slob."

Now that he mentioned it, I saw that he really was sluglike. His whole body seemed to slouch, limbs loose, shoulders slumped. Even his hair fell lazily over one eye.

He went on, "I was fooling around on the computer one day — when I was supposed to be cleaning my room —" he added with a mischievous smile, "and I made a few posters. Just for a gag."

"Some gag," I said, rolling my eyes. "I sure fell for it."

He chuckled. "Never thought anyone would think I meant real slugs." Then he looked at me, perplexed. "But so what if I did? Why do you care about slugs?"

"Because I'm trying to have the *Araneus vampiricus* named the Provincial Arachnid of British Columbia."

"Huh?" He looked at me oddly. "Who are you?"

"I'm Starshine," I said, and explained about the fanged vampire spider and its diet of slugs.

A smile of understanding spread over his face. "So that's why you freaked out when you saw the poster."

"Yeah," I said. "So would you please change the name of your society, before everybody starts saving slugs?"

He waved a hand carelessly. "They won't. Like you said, everybody hates slugs."

"But you never know, Rob, it might become a fad. The slug-saving craze. Who knows how many people have already seen your posters and put up little slug protection zones in their backyards? Oozy, gooey slugs living safe and sound, producing little baby slugs, mounds of squishy, slimy slugs everywhere. Do you want to be responsible for that?"

He looked alarmed. "No way! OK, I'll change the name. But to what? It's got to be good. It's got to really express slugdom."

"How about the Society for the Preservation of Couch Potatoes?"

"Hey, that's good!" He heaved a sigh of relief. "OK, new name. All done. Now can I go back to vegging out?"

"No."

"No?" He sounded dismayed. "Why not?"

"Because those posters are still out there. You've got to take them down and put up some new ones, with the new name. As soon as possible. Like right now."

He looked stricken. "*Work?* Agh. You don't understand. I really am a slug — I mean, a couch potato," he amended when I glared at him. "Just thinking about all that makes me tired."

"But Rob, people are seeing that poster as we speak —"

Just then footsteps came storming up the front stairs. Rob and I turned.

# Chapter Ten

A man and a girl were standing on the doorstep. Both had shiny black hair and brown skin. They were clearly father and daughter. The girl looked about Rob's age, taller than me, shorter than him. In one hand she held a plastic ice cream bucket, in the other, a crumpled piece of paper. She looked furious.

"Are you Rob O'Shea?"

"Yeah."

"Well, you'd just better stop it! Right now! Who ever heard of such a ridiculous thing?"

"Nona, please —" the man said.

Ignoring him, she turned to me. "I suppose you're in on it, too?"

"Stop what?" Rob said.

"In on what?" I said.

She tossed her head and her long ponytail flew from side to side. "The Society for the Preservation of Slugs! Of all the —"

"But —"

"But —"

"You ought to be ashamed, both of you! Those disgusting things. Do you know what pests they are? Do you know the damage they do? Do you care? Of course not. You just —"

"Nona, please, you mustn't yell," her father said, darting us an embarrassed look.

"Hey, wait a minute," I said to her. "I'm not with him!"

"You're not?"

"No!"

She looked suspicious. "Then what are you doing here?"

"Same thing you are — trying to stop him."

"You are? Honest?"

"Honest."

She grinned at me, her teeth white against her dark skin. "Sorry about that." Then she frowned at Rob. "So you're the problem."

"Nona, your manners!" her dad said.

She was unfazed. "Well, he is."

Rob held up his hands. "Hey, I really didn't mean —"

"You didn't mean!" the girl interrupted. "That's no excuse. I suppose you didn't mean to put up your posters, either. Well, you know what? Those charming slimeballs you're trying to save are making my life miserable."

"They are?" Rob said, alarmed. "How?"

"How? I'll show you how!"

She took the lid off the ice cream bucket and pulled out the stem of a vegetable. Hanging from the stem was an orange sack. It looked like a balloon with all the air drained out, only instead of being rubber, this thing was obviously some kind of plant. Or it had been a plant. Now, only the skin remained. It hung there, empty and orange.

"What is it?" I said.

"My prize pumpkin," the girl wailed.

"Your what?" Rob said incredulously. But as we both took a closer look, I saw that the hanging thing was indeed a pumpkin — the collapsed shell of what had once been a pumpkin. Something — or a lot of somethings — had burrowed inside and eaten it from the inside out. She lifted it by the stem, clear out of the bucket, and it stretched three feet. Then she pulled at the sides, and it stretched out just as wide. It would have been huge. But it was empty. Hollow. The ghost of a prize-winning pumpkin.

"Golly," Rob said. "It's … "

"It's … " I said.

"Gone! Destroyed! Annihilated!" the girl yelled, dropping the pumpkin skin back into the bucket and slapping on the lid.

"Nona, please, lower your voice," her dad begged.

"I would have won first prize at the Harvest Fair with that pumpkin," she shouted. "I would have beaten Tamara Benson. Do you know how many years I've waited to beat her? Four, that's how many. Three years ago, she beat me for the biggest begonia. Two years ago, she won for the reddest tomato. Last year, I was sure I had the longest zucchini, but no, she nosed me out by a stem. But this was my year. My pumpkin was going to top anything she could grow. I fed it fish fertilizer. I watered it. I mulched it with rotted hay. It was on track to reach 150 pounds. Until those miserable slimy worms took over."

"Molluscs," I said.

"What?"

"Slugs are molluscs."

"Molluscs, shmolluscs!" she snapped. "They're vile and I hate them." She turned to Rob, finger pointing. "You and your precious slugs —"

"They're not my precious slugs," Rob wailed. "You don't understand. I hate them, too."

She gaped. "You what? You do? Then why … ?"

"I never meant slugs," Rob said in an exasperated tone. "I meant lazy people. People who don't want to do anything. People who just want to lie around."

"You mean couch potatoes?" the girl asked.

"See?" I said to Rob.

He buried his face in his hands. "It was all a huge misunderstanding."

"Misunderstanding!" she shouted. "That's an understatement."

Footsteps sounded in the hall. A woman appeared, tall and slim and red-haired like Rob, but with only half as many freckles. His mom, I guessed. "Rob, what's going on?"

The girl's dad stepped forward. "Oh, I'm terribly sorry, Mrs. —"

"O'Shea."

"Mrs. O'Shea. My daughter has burst in here rather rudely.

Come, Nona, let's go —"

"I'm not going anywhere until he does something about this." She thrust out the paper. Even though it was crinkled, I could make out the words PRESERVATION and SLUGS.

"About what?" Mrs. O'Shea asked.

"Nothing, Mom," Rob said, trying to hide the poster. "I don't think you need to see —"

She grabbed it from the girl's hand.

"Really, Mom, don't worry about it." Rob tried to snatch the poster but his mom held it out of reach.

Mrs. O'Shea read it, then glared at him. "Rob O'Shea, what have you been up to?"

"It was just a joke, Mom —"

"The Society for the Preservation of Slugs, indeed! Of all the crackpot ideas."

Rob squirmed.

"And these poor people thought you meant it?"

Rob squirmed more.

Mrs. O'Shea turned to the girl and her dad. "I'm terribly sorry, Mr. —"

"Patel. Ashok Patel. And this is my daughter, Nona."

"Mr. Patel and Nona." She turned to me. "And you, too, dear —"

"Starshine Shapiro."

"Starshine. I apologize to all of you. It seems that my son has been up to one of his pranks" — she shot him a scathing look — "which he gets up to with great regularity."

"But Mom —"

Mr. Patel broke in, "Oh, no, Mrs. O'Shea, I'm the one who must apologize, for my daughter's behaviour."

"But Dad —"

"No, no, Mr. Patel, Rob was completely out of line."

"No, no, Mrs. O'Shea, Nona came barging in here —"

"Nonsense. If Rob hadn't provoked her —"

"Oh, it doesn't take much to provoke Nona, I assure you."

"Would you care for a cup of tea, Mr. Patel?"

"Yes, thank you. Perhaps it would be good to leave these young people to iron out their ... uh ... misunderstanding."

"I agree." Mrs. O'Shea glared at Rob. "No more funny stuff, Rob."

"Who, me?" he said in an innocent tone.

"Yes, you. And you'll be hearing from me later, young man. Your problem is, you have too much time on your hands. We'll soon fix that."

Rob groaned.

"Mind your temper, Nona," Mr. Patel warned, and followed Mrs. O'Shea down the hall.

Rob, Nona and I stood there facing one another.

"All right," Nona said, "the first thing is to change the name of the society."

"We already did that," I told her.

She shot me an approving look. "Good. What's the new name?"

"The Society for the Preservation of Couch Potatoes."

"Brilliant!" She turned to Rob. "Why didn't you use that in the first place?"

He buried his face in his hands. "I didn't think of it. I wish I'd thought of it. I didn't think anyone would think I meant real slugs. Who in their right mind would think that?" Then he put up his hand. "No, don't tell me —" he began, as Nona and I both yelled, "We did!"

"All right, then," Nona said. "Next, we've got to make new posters. And take down those old ones, before people start saving the little beasts."

I smiled. "Rob and I were just discussing that."

He slumped against the wall. "Wait a minute. You don't get it. I hate work. I'm allergic to work."

Nona's eyes flashed. "My heart bleeds. You made this mess and now you've got to clean it up."

"But —"

"March," Nona said.

Wow, I thought. General Nona.

With a sigh, Rob headed down the hall, his feet dragging. He led us to a bookshelf-lined study. Slumping into a desk chair, he turned on a computer and opened a file. Up popped the dreaded poster. "OK," Nona began, "change 'SLUGS' to —"

But before she'd even finished the sentence, Rob had replaced "SLUGS" with "COUCH POTATOES" all six times it appeared. Then, moving the mouse and tapping the keyboard at an amazing speed, he got rid of the slug and added computer drawings of potato-shaped people slouching on a couch, cartoon potatoes snoozing, others yawning, bubbles coming out of their mouths saying "Veg out!" and "Proud bum!" and

"Slobs unite!" By the time he was done, the poster looked like it had come out of a professional comic book, and it had taken all of a minute and a half.

"Wow!" I said, "you're good."

"You're a genius," Nona said.

"Thanks." Rob blushed, the red blending in with the freckles.

"I thought you hated to work," I said.

"Aw, that stuff's easy," he said with a wave of the hand. "I can do it in my sleep." He paused. "Sometimes I *do* do it in my sleep." He printed out several copies, then sank onto a couch in the study. "OK? Are you guys happy? Now will you leave me in peace?"

"Do you promise to take down the old posters and put up these ones?" Nona asked.

"Do I have to?"

"Yes!" Nona and I said together.

Great sigh. "All right."

"Then we'll leave you in peace," Nona said.

We started heading out of the study when she turned to me. "I never did catch what you were doing here, Starshine. What's your problem with slugs?"

I explained that I was trying to have the *Araneus vampiricus*, the fanged vampire spider, named the Provincial Arachnid.

"Yeah, but what's that got to do with slugs?"

"Well, this spider eats slugs. Only slugs, in fact. So when I heard about the Society for the Preservation of Slugs —"

"It WHAT! It eats slugs? Why didn't you say so in the first place?"

"Well, I —"

"Destroys them? Kills them? Eliminates them?"

"Sucks the slime right out of them," I informed her.

She shrieked. "That is fabulous! That is fantastic! I love them! I want some! How do we do this Provincial Arachnid thing? Convince the government? Get a law passed? Write a letter?"

I shook my head. "Get three thousand people to sign a petition."

"All right, then, let's go! What are we waiting for? Come on, let's start signing up people — now!" She yanked Rob's and my sleeves.

Rob pulled his arm away. "Count me out, guys." He slouched farther down in the couch, sinking into the cushions.

I shook my head. "It's not that easy, Nona. I spent yesterday afternoon going up and down my street and I only got two signatures."

Nona looked daunted — for about three seconds. Then she said, "All right, then we've got to figure out another way. We need a campaign. We've got to let people know how wonderful this spider is. We've got to tell them about the slugs. Gardeners, especially. They'll go nuts. They'll sign in droves. We've just got to get the word out. We need a major blitz. Billboards. Ads … "

I saw what she was getting at. An advertising campaign, like companies do to sell their products. Buy this car. Wear these sneakers. Sign this petition. "Photos," I added excitedly.

"Banners —"

"Posters —"

We both stopped. We both turned to Rob.

He must have known what we were thinking, because he put up his hands. "No way."

"But Rob, you're so good on the computer," I said.

"You're a whiz," Nona added.

"You said it was easy," I pointed out.

"Yeah, but that doesn't mean I want to do more of it. I did my part. I changed the name. I made new posters. I even promised to put them up. That's it. That's more work than I've done all week. Go away!"

"Come on, Rob, we need you," Nona said.

"No."

"You can do it sitting down," I said.

"No."

Nona's face turned a dangerous shade of rosy brown. "Rob, get off your bum and start helping!"

He folded his arms across his chest and stuck out his feet, ankles crossed. "No way. Once a couch potato, always a couch potato. I'm not doing another thing."

"Rob —" Nona yelled.

I could see that she was about to lose her temper. And it wasn't going to help, because in spite of the fact that Rob looked so relaxed he was practically asleep, I could tell his heels were dug in. Hard.

Then I got an idea. A crazy idea. A risky idea. It might work, it might not. But we weren't getting anywhere this way. I pulled Nona out into the hallway. "Listen, Nona," I whispered, "bossing him isn't working. Let's try bargaining with him."

"No way! To heck with him. You and I can do it."

"How? You said yourself we need an advertising campaign. Can you do that computer stuff?"

"No," she admitted.

"Neither can I. We can't make up posters, do pictures, come up with banners, write slogans. But he can. He's brilliant at it. We need him."

"But …" She cooled off a bit. "What do you mean, bargain with him?"

"Well, there must be something he wants. Maybe we can make a trade — his help in exchange for something we can give him. What does he want?"

"To get out of doing work."

"Right," I said. "So maybe if we offer to do some job for him, he'll do the computer stuff for us."

"No way am I doing his work for him, the lazy slob!"

"But Nona, it's the only way. Let's face it, we need his help. And think what a fabulous job he'll do. You saw him on the computer. He's a genius."

Nona scowled. I could tell she really didn't like the idea of bargaining with Rob, but she knew we were stuck. "All right. But the job better not be too big, or the deal is off."

We went back into the study. Now Rob was lying down, his eyes closed, his arms folded under his head, his feet dangling over the end of the couch.

"Rob," I said sweetly, "we've got a proposal for you."

He didn't stir. "Yes?"

Nona made a grumbling noise. Before she could scuttle the whole thing, I said, "We'll make a trade with you. We'll do some of your work — a job or chore or something — in exchange for you doing the computer stuff for the *Araneus vampiricus* campaign. What do you say?"

His eyes opened. "Do some work for me?"

"Mmm-hmm. You pick a job. We'll do it. That's the trade."

Rather more quickly than I'd seen him move so far, he swung his feet around and sat up. A grin split his face. "Now you're talking. All right, let's see. What job do I really not want to do? What job is worth my genius on the computer — I believe you used that word, didn't you? Hmmm … "

Nona tensed and I thought she was going to sock him. I grabbed her arm.

Rob grinned wider. "I've got it. The perfect job."

"What?"

"Painting the backyard fence. My mom's been bugging me all summer. I've been avoiding it all summer. That's my offer."

"Forget it," Nona said, and started to walk away.

Again, I pulled her out into the hall. "Nona, listen —"

"It's ridiculous! Totally out of line —"

"No," I said in a low voice, "it's good for us, don't you see?" "How?"

"It's going to take us a long time to paint the fence. Several days at least."

"That's my whole point!"

"And for every hour we paint, he has to put in an hour on the computer. We'll get tons of advertising stuff. Days' worth. A whole campaign."

A smile spread across her face.

We went back into the study. "You're on, Rob."

He actually got to his feet. We shook hands all around. "It's a deal."

When I got home, I told my mom and dad that I'd met these real nice kids and we were going to be working on a spider project together. That didn't surprise them, since I'm always working on spider projects. Then I said, "Oh, by the way, do you have an old shirt I can use as a painting smock, Dad?"

My dad gave me a funny look. "Painting spiders?"

"Of course not. But painting is part of the project. Along with computer stuff and slugs and gardening and a petition."

My mom rolled her eyes. "I don't even want to know."

# Chapter Eleven

The next day, wearing our dads' old shirts that came down to our knees, Nona and I followed Rob out to the backyard and checked out the fence. It was a typical picket fence — a line of shoulder-high, pointed posts crossed by two horizontal bars. It stretched down one side of the yard, along the back and up the other side.

It was a big yard. It was a long fence.

Rob set down two buckets of white paint and two brand-new paint brushes. Then, with a happy sigh, he flopped down and stuck a blade of grass between his teeth. "Go to it, guys," he said cheerfully. "And do a good job, now. Just let me know when you run out of paint." He leaned back against an apple tree, arms behind his head, and closed his eyes.

Nona looked as if she'd like to smack him, and I felt the same, but we didn't. That wouldn't get us anywhere. Besides, we didn't want to give him the satisfaction of getting us riled up.

We started painting. The paint smelled fresh and clean, it

slathered on creamy and thick, and the new white was dazzlingly bright against the faded old paint. Nona and I smiled at each other. This wasn't so bad.

We each finished our first slat, then stood back to admire our work.

"Good job," Nona said.

"Same to you."

"You've got a spot on your nose."

"Where? Here?" I wiped.

"Now it's a splotch."

I giggled. Who cared if I had a splotch on my nose? This was fun.

But not for long. By about the eighth post, the brushes felt heavy, the paint smelled gross, we were sweating under our smocks and our necks were getting cricks from bending down to paint the undersides of the bars.

"Having fun?" Rob called.

"Yesss," Nona and I both hissed.

Rob smirked.

We continued painting, determined to ignore him. Then a voice broke the silence. "Rob O'Shea, what is going on here?"

We turned and saw his mom. Frowning, arms crossed, she was advancing toward us.

I shot Nona an alarmed look. She shot me one back. If Mrs. O'Shea didn't let us do the painting, Rob wouldn't do our campaign.

Rob looked alarmed, too, probably at the prospect that he might have to paint. He jumped up. "Mom —"

"What is the meaning of this? This is your job. How you conned these poor innocent girls into doing your work —"

"But Mom —"

"— when you should be the one —"

"But Mom —"

I dropped my brush and ran over. "Mrs. O'Shea, it's not what you think."

"Yeah, he didn't con us, we made a trade," Nona added.

Mrs. O'Shea looked like she didn't believe a word of it.

"Honest," Nona said. "Starshine and I are painting the fence in exchange for something we want Rob to do."

I leaned close to Rob's mom. "And believe me, we're getting the better deal."

She looked at me, surprised.

"This is a piece of cake compared to what we're going to make him do," I whispered.

She considered. "Very well, as long as Rob does his part. I'm counting on you two to make sure he does."

Nona and I exchanged a grin. "Oh, don't worry, Mrs. O'Shea, we will."

Rob's mom turned to him with an amused look. "You know something, Rob? I think these girls might be very good for you."

Rob looked slightly ill. Mrs. O'Shea went back inside. Rob flopped back down. "Whew," we all said.

Nona and I continued painting. Twelve posts … thirteen. Our arms ached. The spatters on our skin dried and pulled like scabs. Wisps of hair tickled. Seventeen … eighteen.

Rob raised himself on his elbow and scanned our work.

"You missed a spot," he said, pointing.

"Oh, shut up," Nona growled.

"Well, that's no way to do a good job."

"Oh, shut up," I said.

"You promised my mom —"

Nona picked up her can of paint and held it over him. "Are you going to be quiet now?"

He nodded, wide-eyed.

She came back and we smirked at one another. Then we looked at all the posts still left to do, and our smirks faded.

Wearily, we continued painting. Nona talked about her garden. She told me how she'd tended her pumpkin plant this year — before the slugs came. She'd fed it fertilizer, pulled every weed that threatened it, talked to it…

"What did you talk about?" I said.

"How we were going to win a blue ribbon at the Harvest Fair and rub Tamara Benson's perky little nose in it!"

"You don't like her very much, do you?"

"Are you getting that impression?"

"How come?"

"'Cause she's a showoff, that's why. You know what she did? Last year, after she won her third ribbon, she had a charm bracelet made with charms of her winning plants: a little silver begonia, a tomato and a zucchini. And she's forever jingling it in my face."

"Creep," I said sympathetically.

"And this year she'll get to add a fourth charm," Nona wailed.

"But not next year," I said. "Not when the *Araneus vampiricus* is the Provincial Arachnid."

"Right." She grinned. "Next year things'll be different. I'll show her, that … that … stuck-up snob!"

"Yeah!" I said. "Let's paint!"

And we did. Furiously. For a while. But soon the sun got hotter. We slowed down. Twenty-one … twenty-two. The brushes got heavier. The spatters got itchier. Twenty-nine … thirty.

"My arm's about to fall off," I complained.

Nona straightened up from painting one of the crossbars. "My neck's stuck. I'm going to be looking over my left shoulder forever."

With a contented yawn, Rob stretched lazily. "Aahh, this is the life."

That did it. Nona and I, pretending to scrape off our brushes, flicked paint at him, spattering his legs.

"Hey, watch out! You're getting paint on me."

"Oh, sorry, let me clean that for you, Rob," Nona said, wiping the spatters. Of course that turned them into smudges.

I went to help and accidentally dripped paint on his arm.

"Hey, you're making it worse!"

We tried to hold back the giggles, but a huge snort burst out of Nona. We both hooted.

"Very funny, you guys," Rob grumbled, going off to get a rag soaked in paint thinner. While he cleaned himself off, Nona and I decided we'd had enough for one day. We cleaned our brushes and ourselves. Then Nona grinned mischievously, hooking her arm through Rob's. "Now it's your turn, Rob my boy."

"But — but —" Rob sputtered, "I thought you were going to finish your part first."

"Oh no," I said, "that wasn't the deal. For every hour we put in, you put in one, too. And I figure we worked, what, Nona, two hours today?"

"At least."

"More like two and a quarter."

"But we'll be nice and only call it two."

"This time," I was quick to add.

Rob groaned. We followed him into the study. With a sigh he lowered himself into the chair and turned on the computer. "Well, what do you want?"

Nona and I exchanged a look. "What do you mean, what do we want?" she said. "You're the creative genius. Create!"

"But —"

"The computer stuff is your thing," I pointed out. "We're just painters."

He looked dismayed. "You expect me to come up with the whole campaign?"

"Yes," we both said.

"That's not fair!"

"You expect us to paint the whole fence, don't you?"

Rob opened his mouth to answer, then shut it. He slumped forward, elbows on the desk, chin in hands, not moving. Nona reached out to give him a shake, but I stopped her. I had a feeling he was thinking. It was hard to tell — with Rob, thinking looked a lot like sleeping — but there was something in his shoulders that told me that creative energy was floating around in there somewhere. Sure enough, his fingers started tapping. SLUG, he typed. Then, GARDEN. SPIDER. He stared at those words for a while, moved them around, thought some more. Then, GARDENER. A long pause. Then, a sharp intake of breath, a rattling of keys, and at the top of the page appeared: THE FANGED VAMPIRE SPIDER: THE GARDENER'S BEST FRIEND.

I looked at Nona. She looked at me. We both grinned.

"Rob, that's perfect —" I began, then shut up as cartoon pictures started appearing below the title. A guy in overalls, a straw hat, a spade: a gardener. Then a spider. I'd given Rob a picture of the fanged vampire spider, so this spider had all the right markings, the red and yellow stripes and a pair of luscious black fangs. Smiles appeared on the gardener's and the spider's faces. Cartoon hands reached out to shake. Then he added a bunch of little grey slugs hightailing it out of the garden, darting scared looks over their shoulders.

"Wow!" was all I could say.

"Rob, that's fantastic," Nona said. "How do you come up with up this stuff?"

"Oh, just fooling around." But his cheeks were pink and I could tell he was pleased. He pushed back his chair.

"Where you do think you're going?" Nona said.

"I made you a poster —"

"Yeah, and we painted about thirty slats. Keep your bottom in that seat."

"But —"

"I figure he's up to about, oh, eight posts, right, Nona?" I said.

"Eight?" Rob wailed.

Nona grinned at me behind his back. "Give him ten, Starshine."

I made a big show of being generous. "All right, ten."

With a groan, Rob opened a new file. Fingers poised on keys, he looked out the window. By now, Nona and I knew better than to interrupt. Moments passed. Then: THE FANGED VAMPIRE SPIDER: THE SLUG'S WORST ENEMY. Before our eyes a terrified-looking cartoon slug appeared, grossly puffy and squishy, its antennae curled in fear. It cringed before an enormous *Araneus vampiricus* that loomed over it, baring dagger-sharp fangs.

"Rob, you're terrific," Nona said.

"More! We want more!" I cried.

Rob turned around, stricken. "More?"

"Oh, yeah, you're not done," Nona said. "Now you're up to the point where you said we missed a spot. Remember that, Starshine?"

"Perfectly."

With a groan, Rob turned back around.

Nona and I sat on the couch, leaned back, arms behind our heads. "Aahh," I said, "this is the life."

Rob made a choking sound. Nona and I managed not to laugh. He stretched out in the chair and half closed his eyes. There was a long silence. Finally, Nona jumped up. "Hey, what gives? Do something."

Rob glared. "Leave me alone. We creative geniuses need to connect with our muses."

"Oh, is that what you're doing?" Nona said sarcastically. "Looked like you were dreaming."

Rob grinned. "Hey, you just gave me an idea." He typed: THE FANGED VAMPIRE SPIDER: A VEGETABLE'S DREAM COME TRUE.

He made the letters all puffy, as if they were made of pillows. Then he put in pictures of peas, tomatoes, onions, carrots and pumpkins, drew faces on them and gave them arms, which were draped around each other's shoulders. Last, he gave them all big goofy smiles.

"OK, guys, there you go —"

"Don't even think about it," Nona said.

"You're up to about the twentieth post," I said.

Rob groaned.

"I love watching you work," Nona said. "It's so satisfying."

"Don't say that word!"

"What? W —"

"Agh!"

But even as he said it, he was already creating the next poster. THE FANGED VAMPIRE SPIDER: THE SLUG'S WORST NIGHTMARE. This title was written in a quivery style, as if the letters themselves were quaking with fear. Beneath, a row of slugs sat up in bed, clutching their pillows, eyes bulging, mouths gaping in horror. "No!" "Help!" "Not the Fanged Vampire Spider!" they screamed.

At the bottom of each poster, Rob typed: Sign the petition

to make the *Araneus vampiricus* B.C.'s Provincial Arachnid ... and say DEATH TO SLUGS! Then he printed out several copies of each and we spread them on the desk.

"Wow," Nona said.

"They're awesome, Rob," I said.

"Really?" he said eagerly. Then he seemed to catch himself, and he leaned back with a bored expression. "Can I stop now?"

Nona checked her watch. "What do you think, Starshine? Enough?"

I pretended to think it over. "I suppose that's thirty posts' worth."

Rob turned off the computer. "Man, you two are slave drivers."

Nona and I smiled. "Oh, we're just getting warmed up," she said.

With an exhausted-sounding sigh, Rob lay his head on his arms and collapsed on the desk.

# Chapter Twelve

So it went. Each morning Nona and I painted and got hot and tired and itchy and sweaty, while Rob lay in the shade, saying helpful things like, "Boy, you haven't done very much, have you?" and "A little more on that crossbar there." And each afternoon we sprawled on the couch, saying "Keep 'em coming, Rob old boy," while he slaved over the computer.

The fence got whiter. The pile of advertising stuff grew thicker. Every day, Nona and I got more excited. Soon the fence would be finished. And soon the fanged vampire spider campaign would be ready to hit the streets.

Meanwhile, every few days, when I got home there was a phone message for me. Julie. Miranda. Julie. Roxanne.

Looking at the messages, scribbled in my mom's or my dad's handwriting, I felt elated. How I missed my friends! How great the campaign would go with their help! I put my hand on the phone.

Then I remembered how they'd laughed at me. How they'd plotted behind my back. I took my hand off.

On.

Off.

I didn't return the calls.

It was Nona's and my fifth day of painting. We'd finished the first side and the back of the fence. Only the second side remained.

"What can we talk about?" Nona said to me.

I shrugged. We'd already talked about everything we could think of: school, teachers, sports, movies, soft pretzels with mustard (we both loved them), nail polish (we both hated it), parents, sisters, brothers, pets (Nona had a collie and a parakeet; I had spiders — sometimes), and our most gory cuts and scrapes.

"I don't know," I said. "How I spent my summer vacation."

"Painting Rob O'Shea's fence. Whoop-de-do."

"Last summer."

"Hmm … " She swished her brush, thinking. "Oh, yeah, there was one funny thing that happened. We were camping in Garibaldi Park, my mom and dad and brothers and I. This one day we were hiking along a creek … "

As Nona spoke, I noticed Rob wiggling restlessly under the tree. He'd been like this for several days now, changing positions, getting up to check on our work, lying down again. I'd been wondering what was wrong with him, and now it hit me. He was bored. Bored to tears. It looked as if the fun of lying around and watching us work and razzing us had faded for the old couch potato.

Hah!

" ... So we came around a bend," Nona was saying, "and there was this mama bear with two cubs by the side of a creek." Pausing, she touched up a spot. Out of the corner of my eye, I saw Rob slither toward us. He made a show of examining something in the grass.

Nona went on, "The mama bear growled at the cubs to keep still and they stood at the edge of the creek, leaning forward, watching. She swatted her hand, real quick, and came up with a fish."

Rob edged closer.

"Then one of the cubs, imitating the mother, swatted the water. Only it lost its balance and fell in, face first."

Rob gave up pretending not to listen. He came over and leaned on the unpainted part of the fence.

"And then the other one, thinking it was a game, I guess, jumped in too," Nona finished.

Rob and I burst out laughing.

"That reminds me of when my dad and I were staying in this cabin in the mountains," he said. Absentmindedly, without seeming to be aware of what he was doing, he picked up an extra paint brush that was lying around and dipped it in the paint.

Nona shot me a look. Her eyes were twinkling and her nostrils were going in and out and her mouth was twitching. I could tell she was dying to say something, but I stomped on her foot. If Rob realized what he was doing, he'd stop, and why shouldn't we get a little free help if we could? But it was so funny that a laugh started bubbling out of me, so I turned it into a cough — the phoniest cough I'd ever heard.

Rob gave no sign of noticing. "I was getting wood from the woodshed," he said as he continued painting, "and as I came around the woodpile, my arms full of firewood, I found myself face to face with a bear." He touched up the crossbar, remembering. "For one second, we stared at each other. Then, at exactly the same moment, we both jumped. The bear ran in one direction, and I flung out my arms, dropped all the firewood, and ran in the other direction. My heart didn't stop pounding for an hour, and I bet that bear's didn't either."

We all laughed. Totally unaware, Rob went on painting, stepping back every so often to admire his work. Nona winked at me. I bit my cheeks not to laugh.

As we continued painting, Rob told us about another camping trip, when a bear dug up a bucket of food that Rob's mom had buried in the ground to keep cool. It ate everything in it, including his older sister's make-up, which had somehow got mixed in with the cheese and eggs. They found an empty container of blush and several empty tubes of lipstick. For the rest of the camping trip, they were on the lookout for a bear with rosy cheeks and red lips.

We laughed and told stories and painted. Nona kept elbowing me and I kept snorting, and Rob kept painting. Post by post, we worked our way up the yard. Before we knew it, Rob swiped his brush over the last post. His brush hit air. He looked down. For the first time, he saw — really saw — the brush in his hand. A look of bewilderment crossed his face. "How did this get here?"

Nona and I didn't say a word.

"Did I actually do *work*?" he muttered. "Did I actually enjoy it?" He shuddered. "What's happening to me?"

He looked so dismayed, I felt sorry for him. Patting him on the shoulder, I said, "Don't worry, Rob, it's not so terrible. It was fun, wasn't it?"

A smile crept up his face. "Yeah."

"And look what a great job we did," Nona added, patting him on the other shoulder.

The smile turned into a grin as he surveyed the gleaming white fence. "Yeah, we did, didn't we?" Then his panic-stricken look returned. "I'm losing it. I'd better rest until the feeling passes." He wandered off toward the house.

Nona and I held it in until he was out of earshot.

"Did you see —" she guffawed.

"He-he —" I couldn't finish my sentence.

"Clueless —"

"The look on his face —"

We laughed until our stomachs hurt. While we cleaned our brushes for the last time, we agreed not say anything, tempting though it was. The poor guy's reputation was in tatters. It didn't seem fair to rub it in.

By the time we joined Rob in the study, he'd made a complete recovery. Lounging in the desk chair, he gave a lazy smile. "This is your last chance to squeeze work out of me, you tyrants."

"Oh, but Rob, we'll miss bossing you around," Nona said sorrowfully.

"Yeah," I added, "it's been so much fun."

Rob snorted. "Too bad." He poised his hands over the keyboard and I knew he was thinking about what to do next. Nona and I waited. He set up a series of three ads. At the top of each, in fancy, restaurant menu-style writing, he wrote: TODAY'S MENU: BREAKFAST. TODAY'S MENU: LUNCH. TODAY'S MENU: DINNER. In each ad he drew an *Araneus vampiricus* sitting at a table with a napkin around its neck, a fork and knife in its hands, its tongue slurping out to lick its lips. On the table in front of it was a plate with a slug overturned on its back, a look of terror on its face.

Each spider had a speech bubble coming out of its mouth. The breakfast spider was saying, "I love 'em broiled. I love 'em boiled." The lunch spider was saying, "I love 'em steamed. I love 'em creamed." The dinner spider was saying, "I love 'em roasted. I love 'em toasted."

Nona and I roared with laughter.

"Rob, that's fantastic!" she said.

Blushing, he designed a petition and printed out several copies. Then Nona and I went through the pile. We had posters, signs, banners, ads and petitions.

"A whole advertising campaign," I said with a grin.

We made a list of places where we could take them: garden stores, produce stores, nurseries, feed stores, vegetable stands, 4-H clubhouses. Nona divided the pile into three equal parts.

"What do you think you're doing?" Rob said.

"But Rob —"

"No way!"

"But we need you —"

"Unh-unh. My part's done. I'm through. Quit! Kaput! Finito!"

Just then there was a knock on the door and his mom poked her head around the door. "Oh, hi, girls. Gosh, the fence looks great."

"Thanks, Mrs. O'Shea."

"You're holding my son to his side of the bargain?"

"You bet."

"Good." She turned to Rob and handed him a piece of paper. "Just to help cure you of your couch-potato-itis, Rob, here's a list of errands you can run for me later."

"But Mom —"

"No buts. It's time you got off your you-know-what."

"But Mom —"

"The exercise'll do you good."

"But Mom —"

She was gone. He groaned, then read aloud, "Dry cleaners. Fruit store. Drugstore. Plant nursery. Health food store." He shook his head. "Oh, man, this is going to take hours."

"Rob," Nona said, "did you say fruit store? And plant nursery?"

"Yeah."

I got Nona's drift. "Then you have to go to those places anyway."

"So you might as well drop off some posters and petitions."

"But —"

"The exercise'll do you good," Nona teased, and we both giggled.

Rob threw up his hands. "Oh, all right, but that's the last thing I'll do. The absolutely last thing."

"Except picking up the signed petitions in a few days," Nona said.

"But —"

"Come on, Rob, you might as well. Your mom'll probably have more errands for you to do anyway. Unless she has something else for you to paint," she added slyly.

"No!" He rolled his eyes. "All right, I'll go back and pick up the petitions. But that's the last thing I'll do. The absolutely, positively last thing."

"OK," Nona and I both said, fingers crossed behind our backs.

Each picking up our pile, we agreed to meet back at Rob's in one week's time to see how we were doing.

"Guys," I said, "let's go get 'em."

# Chapter Thirteen

Walking down the street, my arms full of posters and banners, I was pumped. The fanged vampire spider campaign was going to be a smash. People would see the advertisements and they would rush to sign the petitions. It was only a matter of time before we got the 3,000 signatures and British Columbia had its very own Provincial Arachnid.

I turned the corner and came to a playground. Swings, slide, monkey bars. At one end there was a rollerblading rink where kids gathered for pick-up roller hockey games. Walking by, I scanned the crowd, checking to see if anyone I knew was there.

Julie.

She was with some kids at the side of the rink. She had some papers in her hand, and a pen. Her face was turned sideways to me and I could see that she was smiling, talking in an excited way. She didn't see me. I stopped, hidden by the posters I was carrying, and watched. Some kids came off the "ice" and others skated on to take their places. Julie went right over to the new kids and started chatting to them.

She's making new friends, I thought, my heart sinking. She doesn't want to be my best friend anymore. Tears pricked my eyes. Turning, I started walking away. The next thing I knew, an arm was pulling me around, and Julie was grinning at me. "Star!"

How could she act friendly now? Struggling not to cry, I said, "Making new friends?"

"What?"

I gulped. "Aren't my camp friends enough?"

She looked puzzled. "Enough for what?"

"You tell me."

"Star, what are you talking about?"

Breaking my heart was bad enough, but this innocent act was getting me mad. "Don't pretend you don't know, Julie. You guys are all in it together — you and Miranda and Glynnis and all of them — whatever *it* is."

She got a guilty look on her face.

"See! I told you."

"Told me what?" She shook her head. "Star, what's going on? You'd think I'd done something wrong."

"Oh, no, why would I think that? Just because you told them? Nothing wrong with that, is there, Jule?"

"Told who what?"

"Great joke, huh? Everybody thought it was real funny, huh?"

She rolled her eyes. "I have no idea what you're talking about." She gave me a weak smile. "Star, come on, let's watch 'em play."

"No thanks."

Julie stiffened. She looked hurt. Why on earth did *she* look hurt? What did she expect, that I'd jump at the chance to watch her new friends play roller hockey?

She shrugged. "Never mind." Pointing to the stuff in my arms, she said, "What you got?"

"A whole bunch of stuff which, if you hadn't gone behind my back in the first place, I wouldn't have needed at all!"

"Huh?"

This was getting me nowhere. She was still pretending she hadn't betrayed me, that she didn't have some kind of secret with my camp friends, that everything was fine. "Good luck with your new friends, Jule."

"Star!"

I walked away.

When I got home, I felt rotten. I didn't want to see anybody or talk to anybody. I figured I'd go upstairs and rearrange the spiders on my bulletin board. That always made me feel better.

But as I was crossing the living room, I heard a noise, a muffled, whimpering sort of noise that seemed to be coming from the couch. It was Peggy, all curled up, a lump of misery, crying into the cushion.

My first thought was, Forget it, I've got my own problems.

But then she gave a sorrowful hiccup, and I knew I couldn't leave her like that. I put down the advertising stuff and sat beside her. "Hey, what's the matter?"

"K-K-Kirsten," she said into the couch.

"What about Kirsten? What happened?" But I knew already.

"Sh-sh-she's m-m-mean," Peggy sobbed.

"Come here, Pumpkin," I said, then stopped, amazed at myself. I never called her Pumpkin. Only my parents did. But this was a "Pumpkin" situation. I tugged her by the shoulder, toward my lap. "Come on. Up here. Tell me."

Peggy shook her head. "I h-h-hate K-K-Kirsten," she wept into the cushion.

"Come on, Pumpkin. You're making a mess of the couch."

She gave a giggle that turned into a sob, then climbed onto my lap, burrowing her face into my shoulder. Great, I thought, as she transferred her tears and snot to my T-shirt. But I was surprised to see how cuddly she felt.

"OK," I said, "tell me all about it."

She sniffled for a while. "You know how Kirsten and me were best friends?"

"Yeah."

"Well, we're not anymore!" Fresh sobs. "N-now G-G-Gillian is."

"I thought Gillian was a poo-poo," I observed.

A strangled laugh. "M-m-me too!"

She cried some more. My shoulder got wetter.

"Did Kirsten say why she didn't want to be your best friend anymore?"

Peggy shook her head. "She just wouldn't play with me."

"What happened?"

"When I got to pre-school today she was in the sandbox with Gillian. And when I climbed in, she said, 'Peggy, go away. Gillian and I are playing.'"

Peggy sniffled. I could just imagine Kirsten's tone.

"And then?"

"And then, at story time, I went to sit down next to her, and she scooted her bum over, right where I was going to sit, and said, 'This spot is for Gillian. Go sit somewhere else.'"

The little witch.

"And then, at snack-time, Kirsten had a chocolate cupcake with a cherry on top, and she'd promised she'd share with me, but — but —" She started crying again.

"She shared with Gillian," I finished.

Peggy nodded against my chest.

"And then she and Gillian ran away from you on the playground, and whispered secrets about you, and held hands all morning," I went on.

Peggy lifted tear-filled eyes. "H-how did you know, Star?"

I sighed. "It happened to me once."

"It did?" She looked incredulous. "The same thing?"

I nodded.

"Somebody was mean to you?"

I nodded again.

She considered that. "Not as mean as Kirsten, I bet."

"Meaner."

She looked doubtful. "Who?"

"A girl called Patti. A long time ago." And a girl called Julie. Just now.

Peggy cocked her head. "Did you cry, too?"

"Buckets."

She giggled, then grew serious. "It's yucky, isn't it, Star?"

"Sure is." That was exactly how I felt right now. Yucky.

Peggy seemed to think for a minute. "Why did Patti do that, Star? And Kirsten?"

Boy, how do you answer that one? "I don't know, Peggy. Just because, I guess." I paused, then went on, kind of figuring things out as I went, talking as much to myself as to her. "'Cause they have to be the boss and make everybody follow them. 'Cause they have to be the most popular. I don't know why, they just do. And then, when they get tired of you, or they can't boss you around anymore, or they see somebody else they want to boss around even more, they drop you and go to the new person, and that's it for you. They'll drop them, too. You'll see, Peggy. In a little while Kirsten won't like Gillian anymore, and she'll find somebody else."

It wasn't much of an answer, but it was the best I could do.

"She's mean."

"Yup. But tell me, Peggy, were you nice when you called Gillian a poo-poo?"

She blushed. "No," she said with a sheepish look, "but Kirsten started it."

"That's no excuse. Do you want to be like Kirsten?"

"No!"

"Well, then."

She thought about that for a minute. Then her eyes filled with tears again. "B-b-but Star, everybody likes K-K-Kirsten the b-best. And she has such good t-t-toys!"

I held her. "Oh, Peggy, who needs friends who treat you like that?" To my surprise, tears started squeezing out of my own eyes, and, thinking of Julie, I sobbed on Peggy's head.

Peggy turned up her tear-streaked face. "You really feel bad for me, don't you, Star?"

My sob turned into a laugh. "Y-yeah. I do."

Peggy smiled through her tears. "When I'm big, Star, will I be real best friends with somebody, like you and Julie?"

I swallowed, hard. "Yes, Peggy, you will."

She wiped her face on my shirt. This was one T-shirt that was going straight into the laundry.

"OK," she said with a contented sigh.

"OK," I said.

We hugged. Then, grabbing my pile of advertising stuff, I went upstairs, feeling better — and worse — than I did in the first place.

# Chapter Fourteen

Gertie's Garden Garage, said the sign in the window. And it really was a garage, too. Gertie — whoever she was — had taken an old gas station, torn out the gasoline pumps and put up rows of tables, which were covered with plants. And she'd turned the garage part into a glass-covered greenhouse.

I didn't see any cash register or office outside, so I went into the greenhouse to look for Gertie. People crowded the aisles with pots and trays and carts full of plants. I squeezed past a woman with a tray of pansies, a man carrying four jugs of fish fertilizer, a woman with several dangerous-looking garden tools, a man holding a potted tree that was taller than he was, and two old ladies blocking the aisle while they argued about which was the best-smelling rose.

"*Prima Ballerina!*" one said.

"*Sarabande!*" the other yelled.

"*Prima Ballerina!*"

"*Sarabande!*"

Finally I reached the cash register. A woman stood behind

the counter. Curly brown hair stuck out from under a green baseball cap, and a button pinned to her shirt said, GERTIE SEZ: THINK GREEN.

"Are you Gertie?" I asked.

"You got 'er. Gertrude Grantham. And you are —"

"Starshine Shapiro."

"How de do, Starshine? You got a gardening problem?"

"Well, no. I don't even have a garden."

"Oh. Whatcha doing here, then?"

"I wanted to ask if you'd be interested in putting up a poster."

"Gee, I don't know. Not a lot of extra space around here. What's it about?"

"Making the *Araneus vampiricus* the Provincial Arachnid."

She frowned. "Look, kid, I don't know what this Araney-whoozamawhatzit is, but if it's a government thing, forget it. I do enough for them at tax time."

"No, no, nothing like that," I said, holding up a poster. "See?"

Her eyes ran over it. "Fanged vampire spider," she read idly, not really paying attention, " … slug's worst enemy … " Her eyes bulged. "SLUG'S WORST ENEMY! Let me see that!" She grabbed the poster out of my hands. "DEATH TO SLUGS!"

People heard her and started crowding around, jostling to see. The woman with the pansies smashed into the guy with the fish fertilizer, and he dropped one of the jugs on his toe and started hopping around, yelling, "Ow! Ow!" Meanwhile, the two old ladies were slashing everybody with their rose thorns, and the man with the tree nearly got beheaded by a hoe.

"Eats slugs?" somebody said.

"What eats slugs?"

"Oooh, look at those adorable fangs!"

Gertie shouted at me over the crowd: "You bet I'll put up your poster, kid. Right here, beside the cash register. Now, where's that petition?"

I handed her a wad.

Gertie winked. "Come back in a few days, kid. I've got a feeling these'll be full."

Yes! I said to myself, and skipped off to Flossie's Flower Shop. It was the same thing there, and at Plant Paradise, and even at Barney's Books, in the section with gardening books. All the shop owners put up the posters, took lots of copies of the petition, and promised to get their customers to sign it.

By the time I headed home, I'd handed out all my advertising stuff and was nearly out of petitions. I could barely keep my feet on the ground. This was great. We were on our way. It was going to work!

I skipped into the house. My mom and dad were in the kitchen and my mom was jumping up and down, shouting, "You'll never believe who I just got a commission from!"

My dad grabbed her by the sleeves and pulled her down. "Who?"

"The Premier!"

"The Premier of British Columbia? Jack Sherman?"

She started jumping again. My dad caught her and sat her in a chair. "Tell us. You're not getting up until you do." He sat down and I did, too. I had to hear this. The Premier of British Columbia!

My mom laughed. When she'd caught her breath, she said, "OK. You remember, I went into Goddess Grove today to deliver the first three Greek goddesses. Paulie liked Artemis and Eos just fine, but she flipped over Ilithyia."

"You took Ilithyia!" I protested. "She's my favourite. I wanted to keep her." Ilithyia is the goddess of childbirth. My mom had made her pregnant. Very pregnant. Like about to give birth any minute. Her belly was so huge that her bellybutton stuck out.

"Keep her?" my mom repeated, looking at me in surprise. Then she rolled her eyes. "I wouldn't want to give Dad any ideas."

"Joanie," my dad said teasingly.

"What do you mean?" I said. Then I realized. "You mean he might want to ... you mean you might ... another baby?"

They both laughed. "Not likely," Mom said.

"You never know," Dad said. He laughed again but I couldn't tell if he was teasing or not. That would be weird. Neat. But weird.

My mom went on to tell us that she and Paulie were discussing her next batch of goddesses, which were going to be

Japanese, when a man came into the gallery. He looked really familiar, my mom said, but neither she nor Paulie could place him. He wandered around, looking at her sculptures while she and Paulie were talking. They finished and the man came over. Paulie introduced herself and my mom. The man said his name was Jack.

"We were shaking hands," my mom said, "and right at that moment it dawned on me who he was, and it must have dawned on Paulie too, because we both said at once, 'Jack Sherman? Premier Sherman?' and I was pumping away, I must have nearly shaken his arm off —" My mom started laughing, and my dad and I joined in. "— saying, 'Gosh, what do I call you? Your Honour? Mr. Premier? First Minister?' And then I realized I was still holding his hand, I must have been holding it for about five minutes, and I dropped it like a hot potato, and all three of us laughed, and he said, 'For today, just Jack.'"

"What was he doing in Goddess Grove?" my dad wanted to know.

"It's his wife's birthday tomorrow," my mom told us. "He said he'd come over to Vancouver the day before for a meeting with the Mayor, but today he was taking the day off to get his wife a gift. He knew she was into goddesses, so he figured he'd get her one of those goddess pendants. So Paulie helped him pick out a lovely silver one, and then he started asking me about the sculptures, and the next thing I knew we were strolling around the gallery together and I was telling him about each one."

"Wow," my dad said. "Which ones did he like?"

"Well, he liked Chang O, the Chinese moon goddess. He said he liked the way I made her face serene, like the moon. I said that was a lovely thing to say, and exactly what I'd been trying to capture. And he liked Lakshmi, the Indian goddess of prosperity. He said he could use some prosperity right now, the way he was spending money on his wife."

My dad laughed and my mom joined in.

"Anyway, we toured the gallery and then he turned to me and said, 'You know who's missing? Demeter.' And I said, 'The goddess of the harvest.' And he said, 'Right.' Then he told me that he loved to garden, that even though he had scarcely any time, what with his job and all, and travelling so much, when he was home he spent every spare minute puttering in his garden. 'My vegetables are doing very well this year,' he said. In fact, I expect a bumper crop — if those darn slugs don't get everything.' He said he'd been battling the slimy bugs —"

"Molluscs," I said.

"What?" my mom said.

"Molluscs. Slugs are molluscs."

"Oh. Well, anyway, he said he'd been winning the battle so far, and what better way to celebrate than with a sculpture of Demeter, the goddess of agriculture? Maybe she'd bless his garden so he'd actually have something to harvest. He said he had a perfect spot in his office. 'Just give me a call when she's ready, and we'll arrange to have you bring her over to Victoria,' he said."

My mom popped up and started jumping again. "Oh, Pete, I'm so excited!"

He took her hand and started jumping, too. "I'm proud of you, Joanie!" Together, they bounced out of the kitchen.

Cool, I thought, my mom on a first-name basis with the Premier of British Columbia.

Then it struck me. Maybe she could put in a good word with her buddy Jack about the Provincial Arachnid. He could sign it into law, just like that. I wouldn't even have to collect the signatures.

Would that be cheating?

Nah.

Well, maybe a little.

Well, sort of.

Well, yeah, it would totally be cheating.

OK, I promised myself. No asking Mom to go to the Premier. Unless I'm absolutely, totally desperate.

# Chapter Fifteen

About a week later, I made the rounds to pick up petitions. Gertie's Garden Garage was just as mobbed as before. I squeezed my way to the cash register.

"Hi, Gertie," I called over the noise of the crowd. "How'd it go?"

Instead of answering, she grinned and handed me a fistful of sheets. Rows of names marched down the columns. Beautiful, lovely names, line after line of names. Some people had written comments in the margins: "Go, *Araneus vampiricus!*" "Where can I get one of these things?" "Me first!"

"You should see people's faces when they come up to the counter and see the poster," Gertie said.

Just then, a woman walked up, balancing two trays of plants, one in each hand. Gertie winked. "Here's Mrs. Pulaski, one of my regulars," she whispered. "Watch."

Mrs. Pulaski put the trays on the counter and opened her purse. "I'm so glad you still had some nasturtiums, Gertie," she began, then noticed the poster. Her eyes grew wide. "Slug's worst enemy!" she shrieked. She leaned across the counter.

"Where's the petition? Where is it?"

Gertie shoved a clipboard at her. Mrs. Pulaski grabbed it and scribbled her name. "The minute that spider thing gets named the Provincial Arachnid, you let me know, OK, Gertie? The minute!"

"Sure thing, Mrs. Pulaski."

The woman left. "See? What'd I tell you?" Gertie said.

All I could do was grin.

It was the same at the other places. Flossie's and Plant Paradise each had several filled petitions. But the biggest surprise came at Barney's Books. I hadn't thought much would happen at a bookstore, but Doug, the guy in charge of the gardening section, handed me three full sheets and took four more blank ones. "Our customers loathe slugs," he said proudly.

On my way out, I stopped in the reference section and looked up "loathe" in a dictionary. "Hate," it said. "Despise. Detest."

"Yes!" I yelled when I got back out on the street.

At home, I did the math. The 54 from Gertie's Garden Garage, plus 37 from Flossie's Flower Shop, plus 25 from Plant Paradise, plus 60 from Barney's Books, made … 176. Wow! I couldn't wait to hear how many Nona and Rob had.

"Well?" I said to them. The three of us were in campaign headquarters — Rob's study.

Nona gave the thumbs-up sign. "I got 24 from my 4-H Club. Everybody signed, except Tamara Benson, of course, who said" — Nona made her voice real whiny — "'I don't need some stupid spider to help me grow prize-winning vegetables.'" Nona frowned. "I'll show that little —"

"Nona," I said gently. "The signatures?"

"Oh, yeah. Sorry." She consulted her list. "On top of that, I got petitions to friends in the Richmond, Surrey and Langley 4-H Clubs. They all have meetings this week. So I don't know yet, but that should bring in at least 100 more. Plus I got 17 at Southside Feeds and 23 at Seed Sensation. So that makes 64."

"Super," I said.

"Wo —" Rob began, then stopped abruptly. "Never mind."

Nona and I exchanged a smirk.

"How about you, Rob?" Nona said.

"Forty-six at Plowshares Co-op, 19 at the Fruit Palace and 58 at Ned's Nursery."

Nona was scribbling away. "One twenty-three. Wow, you doubled me, Rob."

"Excellent," I said.

He shrugged, trying not to smile.

"Starshine?" Nona said.

I gave them my totals.

"Holy cow," Nona said.

"A bookstore," Rob said. "Who'd a thunk it?"

"Oh, they loathe slugs," I said coolly.

"That makes …" Nona scribbled, " … 363."

"Three hundred sixty-three!" I jumped up, punching my

arm in the air. "That's awesome, you guys!"

Nona jumped up, too, eyes flashing. "You're not kidding, Starshine. We're going to do this. I can feel it. But this is only the beginning." She raised her finger. "We can't slacken off. Can't slow down. Can't let up." She started pacing. Her pony-tail swished. "We've got to keep on going. Keep pounding the streets. Keep hitting the stores." She stopped, pointed at herself. "I'll check back with my 4-H Clubs." Pointed at me. "Starshine, you take posters to all the vegetable stands on Main Street." Pointed at Rob. "Rob, you —"

"Take that finger away!"

Nona looked at him. "Huh?"

"I'm not doing any more! Not one more thing."

"Now, listen —" Nona began.

Rob put up his hand like a cop stopping a car. "No, *you* listen. Gathering petitions was the last thing. The absolutely, positively last thing. Remember?"

"You can't quit in the middle," Nona yelled.

"Oh, yes, I can."

I tugged Nona's arm. Giving her a let-me-handle-it look, I said sweetly, "But Rob, you've done such a great job so far."

"But —"

"And your posters are such a smash," I purred. "People are absolutely blown away by them. Today this lady, Mrs. Pulaski, nearly dumped her nasturtiums, she was so excited."

"Really?" A smile crept up his face.

"And the other day a woman said the spider's fangs were adorable."

"Really?"

Nona seemed to catch on. "Yeah, Rob," she crooned, "at Seed Sensation, they said the little slugs clutching their pillows was the cutest thing they've ever seen."

"They did?"

"So don't you want to go back to the stores and see how your posters are doing?" I went on smoothly. "And hear people say how wonderful they are?"

"How creative you are?"

"What a genius you are?"

He wavered. He hesitated. He threw up his hands. "Oh, all right, if it'll get you guys off my back. One more time. One. Single. Uno. But this is the last thing. The absolutely, positively, totally last thing. Got that?"

"Got it."

Nona and I winked at each other.

Our house was overflowing with library books on Greek mythology. Sketches of Demeter were taped all over the kitchen wall. Each design was different. In one, my mom had portrayed the goddess as an eggplant, with vines sprouting out of her head. In another, Demeter was a fat, jolly woman, like Cinderella's cartoon fairy godmother. In yet another, Demeter's face was made of different vegetables: a pumpkin for the head, tomatoes for eyes, corn for teeth, spinach for hair, squash for ears. If you cooked her, you would have a full-course meal.

Sketches went up and sketches came down. Sometimes my mom would tape up a fresh bunch of drawings, turn her back on them and then whirl around, as if she were sneaking up on them and could trick the right one into showing itself. Her eyes would dart back and forth. Then, with an anguished cry of "These stink!" she'd tear them all down and reach for her sketchbook.

It's always like this when my mom's working out a new design. She comes up with all kinds of ideas and trashes them as fast as they appear. She paces back and forth. She stands for hours, looking at one design, going, "Yes … Yes? … No … Yes?" She's miserable until she finds something that works just right — she calls that moment "giving birth." Once she's given birth, she's fine, but until then, watch out. Peggy and my dad and I have learned to bring her lots of cups of tea and to agree with whatever she says.

"This design might work."

"Yes, Mom."

"This design is the worst thing I've ever come up with."

"Yes, Mom."

Over the years, we've had many tense days at our house waiting for my mom to give birth, but these were some of the tensest ones ever. Maybe, I thought, we needed to get Ilithyia back.

Then one day …

"Hallelujah!" my mom cried, flinging up her arms. She was surrounded by a sea of crumpled paper, staring at a picture on the wall.

"I think we've given birth," my dad whispered to me.

Peggy and I crossed our fingers.

My mom beckoned us over. "This is it, guys. This is Demeter. Full, round, and fertile. Humble, but noble. Ripe, but not overripe. It speaks of abundance. It speaks of bounty. It speaks of vegetables. Organic, of course. The Premier will love it. … Do you think he'll love it? Is this a Demeter a Premier could love? Be honest, now, I can take it."

My dad, Peggy and gathered around. There were a lot of black lines on the paper. Swirling lines. Wiggling lines. Bold lines. One section reminded me of a watering can. Or was it a wheelbarrow? I didn't see any goddesses, though I did see something I was pretty sure was a zucchini.

My mom waited. The silence lengthened.

Peggy said, "What's a Premier?"

I said, "Those lines are really … black, Mom."

My dad put his hand on my mom's shoulder. "Joanie," he said, "the Premier is going to fall head over heels for this Demeter."

"Hallelujah!" my mom said again. Carefully, she removed the paper from the wall and, clasping it to her chest, walked to her studio.

Peggy and my dad and I turned to one another. "Hallelujah!"

I was as ecstatic as my mom. The signatures were rolling in. Four hundred fifty-three … five hundred eighty-one … Every 4-H Club signed. Everybody who shoppped at Gertie's Garden Garage signed. Doug, the guy at Barney's Books, told me that the petition had even sparked sales of gardening books. "Lots of people had given up on gardening, Starshine," he said. "Defeated by slugs. Your petition has given them renewed hope."

Each week, at our check-ins, when Nona read out the new, astounding, wonderful total, she and I whooped and hollered. One time Rob even started yelling, "Go, *Araneus vampiricus*! Go, *Araneus vampiricus*!" until Nona and I looked at him and he blushed and shut up. And each week when we sweet-talked him into keeping on making the rounds, he said, "This is the absolutely, positively, totally, completely last thing."

"Sure, Rob."

"The absolutely, positively, totally, completely, final, 100 percent last thing."

"Sure, Rob."

Along about the second week in August, though, I noticed a change. An alarming change. The names were still coming in, but not as fast. One week the take at Flossie's Flowers was 36, the next 28. One week Gertie had two full petitions for me, the next, only one. Rob and Nona were bringing in less, too. Nobody talked about it, but we all knew it was happening. Even Rob looked worried.

The next time I went to Gertie's, there wasn't even one petition full. "Gertie, what's the matter?" I said. "Doesn't anybody like the *Araneus vampiricus* anymore?"

"Hey, kid, it's not that," she said. "It's just that pretty much everybody who shops here has already signed. There's only so many gardeners, you know. I figure you've hit all of mine that you're going to."

Yikes.

One morning I woke up and looked at the calendar. August seventeenth. Only two more weeks of summer vacation. Once school started, it would be harder to make the rounds, harder to collect the names. What were we going to do?

At the next campaign meeting I said, "Face it, guys. We're slowing down. At this rate, we're not going to make it by the end of the summer."

"Sure we will," Nona said. "We're out there. We're going strong. Heck, we've got 624 signatures."

"But it's not enough," I said. "Each week we get fewer. We're fading."

"We're doing our best!"

"I know," I said grimly. "That's the problem. Our best isn't good enough."

I sighed. Rob sighed. Nona didn't sigh. She got to her feet and started pacing. "All right, then, we're having a setback. So are we going to give up? No. What we need is a new boost. A new push."

"What we need is a whole bunch of new gardeners," I said. "Only there is no bunch of new gardeners. We've already reached them all."

A smile spread across Nona's face.

"What?" I said crossly, wondering what there was to smile about.

"Harvest Fair."

"Huh?" Rob and I said together.

"Remember? I told you about it. It's where they give out the blue ribbons for the biggest vegetables and flowers."

"Oh, yeah," I said glumly. "So what?"

Nona was still smiling. "It's the biggest farm fair in British Columbia, that's what. It's held in South Van every summer. Thousands of people go. A whole bunch of new gardeners. And it's this weekend. If the three of us —"

"Hold on a minute," Rob said. "Hold on just one minute —"

"But Rob —"

"I've done enough!" Rob counted off on his fingers. "I've changed the name of my society. I've changed my poster. I've created a whole advertising campaign. I've been dropping off and picking up petitions for weeks. And now you expect me to go some stupid farm fair? Forget it!"

"But Rob, it's a terrific fair," Nona said. "There's more than just vegetable competitions, there's also prizes for the biggest pig, the heaviest horse and the cow that produces the most milk —"

"No way."

"— and blue ribbons for the handsomest rooster and the hen that lays the biggest egg —"

"Not a chance."

"— and a dog show, with all kinds of fancy breeds, and you get to see a sheepdog herd real sheep —"

"Not in your wildest dreams."

"— and a pie-eating contest —"

"N — what did you say?"

"A pie-eating contest."

He broke into a freckle-crunching grin. "Why didn't you say so in the first place? I love pie. I've always wanted to enter a pie-eating contest. What kind do they have?"

Nona rolled her eyes. "How do I know? Blueberry, apple, peach — who cares? The pie-eating contest is beside the point, the point is —"

"No, it's not! Blueberry. Do they really have blueberry? I love blueberry pie. I could eat a hundred of them. I'll win, easy. Wow, I can't wait. When did you say it was?"

"This weekend. And eating pie isn't the reason we're going, Rob. We're going to help Starshine. We're going to get signatures."

"You're going to get signatures. I'm going to eat pie."

Nona and I both gave him dirty looks. He held up his hands. "OK, OK, I'll get signatures. But I'm definitely entering the pie-eating contest."

"Fine." Nona turned to me. "Now, here's what I'm thinking. We need to make a big splash, right?"

"Right."

"Right. And we'll get our chance at the end of the day. That's when everybody gathers at the bandstand for the presentation of the ribbons. Thousands of people. A ready-made audience. You can make a speech, Starshine. My Auntie Bree is one of the fair organizers and I'm sure she'll let you. You tell them about the fanged vampire spider, and then the three of us'll circulate with petitions. Everybody'll sign. Trust me. We're talking about people who hate slugs."

My throat suddenly went dry. "Make a speech?"

"Yeah."

"Over a loudspeaker?"

"Sure."

"With a microphone?"

"Yup."

"Me, talk to thousands of people?"

"Why not?"

I closed my eyes. I saw a sea of faces. Unh-unh. No way.

"Uh ... I don't think ... that is ... I've never ... Couldn't you do it, Nona? You'd be much better than me. After all, you're a gardener. You know how to talk gardener language. And you know people there. They're your friends.

Besides, you're older. And smarter. And braver."

Nona shook her head. "That doesn't matter. You know spiders, Starshine. You know the *Araneus vampiricus*. You know what to tell people. All that stuff about paralyzing slugs and sucking out their insides. You make it sound so good. That's what we need. Right, Rob?"

"Huh? Boysenberry, maybe?"

"Rob!"

"Oh — sorry. No, really, Starshine, Nona's right. You'd do a great job. You'd convince people."

"You really think so?" I said.

"Absolutely." He licked his lips. "Cherry? Rhubarb?"

"ROB!"

# Chapter Sixteen

A huge banner hung over the entrance to the fairgrounds:

## WELCOME TO THE HARVEST FAIR!
### Harvest a Bushel of Fun!

Rob and I were greeted by a swirl of smells: barnyard and hay, fresh baking and buttery popcorn, the hot smell of the dusty earth baking in the sun. And people were everywhere, parents tugging kids to tables of prize jams and jellies, kids tugging parents to pony rides, farmers in overalls and cowboy hats, teenaged girls leading skittish horses.

"First things first," Rob said, pulling me over to an information table.

"But Rob, we're supposed to meet Nona at the prize vegetable booth," I said.

"I know, I know. Just a minute." He leaned toward a woman sitting at the table. "Hi, can you tell me what time the pie-eating contest is? And where?"

She looked him over. "Thinking of entering, are you?"

"Planning on winning."

She smiled. "Oh, cocky young thing, eh? Starts at noon, back behind the prize vegetables. That-a-way." She pointed across the fair.

"Thanks." Rob started to turn away, then turned back. "Say, do you happen to know what kind of pie they have?"

"Rob," I said impatiently. Nona was going to be wondering where we were.

"One minute."

The woman was consulting a sheaf of papers. "Well, let's see, they alternate every year. Last year it was cherry, as I recall. This year I believe it's blueberry … or is it rhubarb?" She flipped a page, ran her finger down. "Pies … pies … yes, blueberry."

"Yes!" Rob yelled. He grinned at her. "Blueberry's my favourite. I'll win for sure."

She smiled. "That's what they all say."

I tugged Rob away and we began to search for the vegetable booth. But it wasn't so easy to find. First we walked past tables and tables of sparkling jams and jellies, each with a frilly cloth cap and a checkered label. Then we found ourselves in a series of barns, passing roosters with turquoise and scarlet feathers … huge workhorses with hairy feet the size of dinner plates … pigs shaped like old-fashioned bathtubs, long and rounded with short, curvy legs …

Finally we made our way out of the barns and came to a long table. A small tree with curly leaves sat on it. Then I took a good look and saw that it was broccoli.

"This must be the place," I said.

"There you are!" Nona said. "Come and see." Proudly, as if she'd grown them herself, she showed us the prize-winning vegetables. There was a tomato the size of a grapefruit. A cabbage the size of a watermelon. A carrot as long as my arm.

Just then a forklift pulled up, carrying an enormous pumpkin. It was the size of an oven. A girl with a perky blonde ponytail was walking alongside it. It didn't take any great detective work to figure out who she was. The driver stopped the forklift beside the table, and he and another man wrestled the pumpkin off the lift and onto the ground. Then, in a cloud of dust, the forklift rumbled away.

I shot a look at Nona. She looked stricken.

Tamara rested her elbow on her pumpkin. Her charm bracelet jingled. "Too bad about your pumpkin, Nona," she said in a phony voice.

Beside me, I felt Nona stiffen. "Congratulations, Tamara," she managed to say.

Rob and I each grabbed one of her hands. For a moment I imagined pushing the pumpkin over onto Tamara. It would have flattened her. You would have to scrape her up with a spatula. It was a very satisfying image.

"Come on, Nona," I said gently.

"Don't torture yourself," Rob whispered.

We led her away.

"Next year, Nona," I said, squeezing her hand.

"Yeah." She brightened. "And then watch out, Tamara Miss Charm Bracelet Benson!"

"That's the spirit," I said.

"Hey, guys, it's time for the pie-eating contest," Rob said. He rubbed his belly. "And I'm ready."

"You're really going to do it?" Nona said.

"You bet. And I'm going to win, too. I haven't eaten anything all day, just to make sure I'm good and hungry."

"Big mistake," Nona whispered to me. She led us behind the vegetable stand and a delicious fragrance of crust and berries wafted toward us. In the shade of a spreading tree stood a long table covered with a green-and-white checkered tablecloth. About twenty blueberry pies and several pitchers of water and drinking glasses spread out, and a dozen stools stood behind the table.

A man with a megaphone was calling, "Come one, come all, try your hand at pie! How big is your appetite? How many can you eat? Two? Three? Four? Take the challenge. Delicious pie, come one, come all."

Lots of people came by and sniffed the pies and licked their lips, but in the end only four contestants entered: Rob; a big beefy guy in a muscle shirt and cowboy hat; a very wide woman with chubby, rosy cheeks; and a skinny man in a button-down shirt and a worried expression.

"All right, friends," the announcer said, "take your seats. The rules are simple. When I say go, you start eating. Knife, fork, hands, whatever you like. You've got exactly three minutes. At the end of that time, whoever has eaten the most wins. The prize is a half a dozen blueberry pies."

With a confident grin, Rob pointed at the blueberry pies,

stacked off to the side, as if to say, They're already mine. The announcer said, "Ready — set — go! May the best stomach win."

Forkfuls, spoonfuls, handfuls of pie. Oozing blueberries, chunks of crust, purple syrup. Quarters, halves, whole pies began to disappear.

"Go, Rob, go! Go, Rob, go!" Nona and I chanted. And boy, was he going. He started with a fork but soon switched to his hand. Blobs of purple stained his T-shirt. His first pie vanished.

"Yay, Rob!" we shouted.

Starting the second pie, he began to slow down. Smaller bites. Sips of water. He paused to burp. A look of distaste began to spread over his face.

Meanwhile, the others were going at it. The woman broke off hunks of pie with her hand and shoved them in. The beefy guy held a pie plate up to his face and gobbled. The skinny guy went at it daintily with a knife and fork, slow but steady.

"One minute gone," the announcer yelled.

"Come on, Matilda!"

"Go, Charlie!"

"That's it, Solly!"

"Eat, Rob, eat!"

But Rob, despite his excellent start, was definitely falling behind. By the time he was halfway through the second pie, his eyes were squeezed shut as if he couldn't bear the sight of another berry. There were long pauses between bites, as if he had to psych himself up each time.

"He's losing it," Nona whispered.

The beefy guy started wolfing down his third pie. Blobs of crust and berries were plastered to his chin. The woman was about a slice behind him. The skinny guy just kept eating, bite after methodical bite.

"Two minutes!"

Rob lifted the last bite of his second pie. He stared at it. He opened his mouth. He closed his mouth. The bite fell down. Rob clamped one hand over his mouth and the other hand clutched his stomach. He lurched to his feet, knocking over his stool, and bolted.

"Now he's really losing it," Nona said.

"Happens every year," someone behind us said. "Some kid with big eyes wolfs 'em down — then chucks 'em up."

"Waste of good pie," someone else said.

"You've got to train," the first speaker said. "Work up to it. Like Solly."

They were right. The skinny guy had four empty pie tins in front of him and was partway through his fifth. The woman got halfway through her fourth and then threw up her blueberry-stained hands in defeat. The muscle man glanced over at Solly's pile, reached for a fifth pie and frantically started chowing down.

"Time's up!"

Calmly Solly put down his knife and fork and wiped his lips. The beefy guy lifted his face from his pie. There was purple mush on his chin and cheeks, and up his nostrils, not to mention all over his shirt.

"Gross," I said.

"And the winner is … Solly Bernstein! For the third year in a row! Congratulations, Solly!"

The crowd burst into cheers. "Thank you, thank you." The champion nodded at the applause, then picked up the stack of blueberry pies. "These'll make a swell snack later on," he said, and marched proudly away.

"My God," Nona said as we walked away. "Makes me nauseous just to think of all that pie."

"Speaking of which, you think Rob's OK?"

"Yeah, he'll be fine. Once he gets rid of it all, which he's probably done by now."

"Poor guy."

"How much do you want to bet he can't stand the colour blue for a very long time?"

We laughed.

"Ladies and gentlemen," a voice crackled over a loud-speaker, "the ribbons will be awarded in five minutes in front of the bandstand."

"Come on," Nona said, pulling me by the arm, "we've got to find Auntie Bree. She said you could make your speech after the prizes were awarded."

"But … but …"

"No buts. You'll be fine."

"But … but …"

The crowd grew thicker as we approached a small stage with a canvas roof over it. Nona dragged me around the side and introduced me to a beautiful woman in a purple sari.

"So you are the friend with the wonderful news," she said, shaking my hand. "Splendid, splendid! Anything to get rid of those disgusting insects —"

"Molluscs," I said.

"Eh?"

"Molluscs. Slugs are molluscs."

"You don't say. Well, Starshine, as soon as I finish presenting the ribbons, I'll introduce you. I assure you, this crowd will be very receptive. Everyone here loathes slugs."

She squeezed my hand, then dashed up three steps to the stage and lifted a microphone from a stand.

"Nona, I can't."

"Yes, you can."

A wave of applause sounded as one of the winners was announced.

"I'll bomb."

"You'll be fine."

More applause.

"But —"

"And now, I'd like to introduce Starshine Shapiro. Starshine has come with an exciting announcement for us. Starshine?"

Auntie Bree beckoned. Nona shoved. Like a robot I climbed the three steps. Auntie Bree handed me the microphone. It was heavy. It dipped. It screeched. People covered their ears.

"Just hold it still," Auntie Bree whispered. "Speak nice and clear."

She left me. I looked out over a sea of faces. Moms and dads, teens and toddlers, grannies and grandpas, all staring at me.

Nona had slid around to the front. She gave me the thumbs-up sign.

"Uh ... hello ... " I said into the microphone. Lo-lo-lo, echoed my voice. There was a funny delay and I heard everything I said a moment later. "Uh ...  my name is Starshine Shapiro ..." Ro-ro-ro ... "And ... uh ... I came to talk to you — that is, the reason I'm here ...  you see, it's an important arachnological project ..."

People started milling around. Muttering. Yawning.

"It's about this spider, which you've probably never heard of ... "

People shifted restlessly. I'm boring them, I thought in a panic. I'm losing them.

I gripped the microphone tighter. "We used to think it was extinct, but I'm happy to tell you ... "

Out of the corner of my eye I saw Rob squeezing through the crowd. He joined Nona at the front. He looked pale but at least he was alive — which was more than I could say for myself right then. He caught my eye, then made a slashing motion across his throat. I thought he meant, *Kill it! Stop! You're bombing! Get out of there!*

I went to put the microphone back on its stand, but Rob shook his head and made the slashing motion more violently. Then I saw that he was mouthing something. What was he saying? I peered at him. Death, he seemed to be saying.

Death?

Then I got it.

I lifted the microphone to my lips. "Death to slugs!" I shouted.

The crowd came alert. "Death to slugs!" several people shouted back.

"Death to slugs!" I yelled again.

"Death to slugs!" roared several hundred voices.

"Death to slugs!" They were responding!

"DEATH TO SLUGS!" a thousand voices echoed.

Wow! What power I had!

I gripped the microphone. "Yes, death to slugs," I repeated, "and I know the way!"

"Tell us!" someone shouted.

"Yes, there is a way — and the way is a spider."

"A spider?" several people murmured.

"Yes, a spider called *Araneus vampiricus*. The fanged vampire spider."

"Yikes!" several voices said.

"Don't worry," I said, holding out my other hand for calm. "The *Araneus vampiricus* is completely harmless — to people. It eats —" I paused for effect. A thousand faces were turned toward me, waiting for my pronouncement — "SLUGS!"

"Hooray!"

"Yes, it eats slugs. Only slugs. Devours them. Obliterates them. Dissolves their insides and slurps it up like soda."

"Hooray!"

"Now, do you want the fanged vampire spider to multiply,

to breed, to come and live in your garden?"

"YES!"

"Do you want the fanged vampire spider to be named the Provincial Arachnid of British Columbia?"

"YES!"

"Then all you've got to do is sign this petition." I held up my clipboard to show them. "Rob and Nona — put up your hands, guys — and I will be coming around with petitions. Sign your name, help us protect the *Araneus vampiricus*, and say death to slugs!"

They clapped. They cheered. They whistled. I handed the microphone back to Auntie Bree. Then I began to shake.

"You were great!" Rob said, running up and punching me in the arm.

"I was?"

"Yeah, you were!"

"Told you," Nona said.

I broke out into a sweat. "I can't believe I did it."

"You sounded like a preacher up there, Starshine," Rob said. "Sister Starshine. 'I have the way! The way is a spider. Glory hallelujah!'"

I laughed. "I was bombing, big-time. You saved me, Rob."

"Well … " he blushed.

I thought of the way he'd encouraged me. The way he hadn't let me blow it. The way he'd showed up, not just today but for the last several weeks.

"Hey, Rob, can I ask you a question?"

"Sure."

"What's going on?"

"What do you mean?"

"With you," I said. "With the campaign. I thought you didn't care."

Pink cheeks. "I don't!"

"Oh, come off it. You've been busting your butt for weeks."

Pinker. "You guys made me."

"Oh, sure," Nona said. "We really had to twist your arm."

"Well…"

"You haven't been much of a couch potato lately, Rob," I teased.

He threw up his hands. "Oh, all right, I admit it. I'm pumped. I want the little guy to win." He shook his head. "A spider. I can't believe I'm all worked up about a spider. But you know what? It's fun! Doing all this stuff is a hoot." He stopped, shook his head. "I don't know what's come over me." Grimaced. "You've got to promise me something."

"What?" we both said.

"Not to tell my mom. She can't know. She'll give me all kinds of stuff to do. It'll be horrible!"

"Your secret is safe with us," I said.

"Thanks."

We grinned at each other.

"Well, what are we waiting for?" Nona said. "Let's go!"

We fanned out into the crowd. People stood in line to sign. Page after page filled up with signatures. Finally, the crowd began to thin, and Nona, Rob and I found each other. Rob and I counted names and Nona tallied.

"Five hundred thirty ... 40 ... you're not going to believe this, guys ... 50 ... 60 ... 570 signatures — in one afternoon!"

"Wow!" I said.

"Plus the 624 we already had ... " Rob said.

"Makes ... " Nona scribbled. "1,194!"

"Holy cow!" I said.

"Awesome!" Rob said.

"We broke 1,000, you guys!" Nona yelled.

The three of us smashed together for a group hug, jumping around in a circle. "Hooray!" we hollered. "Hooray!"

# Chapter Seventeen

By the time I got home, all the excitement of Harvest Fair had faded and reality had hit. One thousand one hundred ninety-four signatures was a lot, a heck of a lot, but it wasn't enough. Not nearly enough. School would start in a little over a week. Gardening season would be over and all the gardeners would put away their hoes and watering cans for another year and forget about how much they hated slugs. The whole project would die. It all would have been for nothing. British Columbia still wouldn't have a Provincial Arachnid.

I trudged up the kitchen steps. School. That reminded me of another problem. Julie. What was I going to do about her? How could I get through grade six without my best friend? She'd have all those new friends I'd seen her making at the playground, and I'd have no one.

I opened the kitchen door. My mom was on the phone, her back to me. "Fine ... two o'clock ... yes, my whole family ... OK, 'bye, Jack."

She hung up, then whirled around. Splats of clay dotted her face and hair, her work apron was smeared with the stuff, and she wore a huge grin.

"Star, guess what. I finished Demeter!"

"You did? That's great, Mom." I tried to sound cheerful. "Did she come out OK?"

"She came out great!" She laughed. "At least, I think she did. I can never tell. One minute I think she's awful; the next, I think she's the best thing I've ever done."

I looked around.

My mom waved her hand. "She's already packaged up. We're going to Victoria tomorrow, to present her to the Premier."

"That's nice — *we're*?"

"Sure, I've told him about all of you, you and Daddy and Peggy. Won't that be fun, meeting the Premier?"

"Yeah, sure."

She peered closely. "Something the matter?"

"No, nothing."

"Starshine ..."

"No, really, Mom." I managed a weak smile. "I was just ... uh ... thinking about school starting."

My mom laughed. "Don't worry, honey, there's still lots of time for fun before then."

"Yeah, I guess."

She hugged herself. "God, I'm glad that's done." She looked at her hands. "I'm a mess. I think I'll have a nice long bath and soak the clay out of my skin."

We both started out of the kitchen. The phone rang. She answered. I paused in the doorway. "Hello? … Oh, hi J —" She stopped abruptly. "She's right here — What? … Oh, OK." She listened for a while. "You've been what? …  No, we didn't know." Then she said, "Hold on a minute." She put her hand over the phone and yelled, "Pete, pick up the extension!" Then she put the phone to her ear again. "Pete, you there? You've got to hear this." She listened again, an odd smile on her face. Then she noticed me standing there. "It's not for you, Starshine."

The way she said it clearly meant, Go away. I walked out of the kitchen. But I couldn't help wondering what was going on. "She's right here," my mom had said. Who else could that be but me? But it wasn't for me. Who was it? And what was that funny smile for?

As I started upstairs, I heard my mom say, "Tomorrow … Premier's office … two o'clock … "

Something to do with Demeter?

Oh, well, who cared? Between failing in my spider campaign and losing my best friend, I had enough to worry about. More than enough.

I love ferries. I've always loved ferries. I love their gleaming white bulk. I love the rocking motion. I love the little tables with raised edges that keep your dishes from sliding off. Most of all I love the foghorn, the delicious terror that strikes when it booms without warning.

But on this ferry ride I was miserable. I kept thinking about the ferry ride two months ago, when my class went to the Royal British Columbia Museum. The junk food. The Checkers. The singing and teasing on the bus. The discovery that there was no Provincial Arachnid, and my decision to do something about it. And, most of all, Julie saying to me, "Hey, kiddo, when have I ever let you down?"

Everything had changed since then. Sure, I'd made new friends. Rob and Nona were great. They'd come through for me like champs. We'd had a lot of fun together. But they weren't Julie. Or Glynnis or Priya or those guys. It wasn't the same. How could it be? No one could replace your closest friends, no matter how nice or helpful they were.

And besides, in spite of Rob and Nona's help, the *Araneus vampiricus* still didn't have a hope in — well, you know what.

With those cheery thoughts, the ferry ride went by, and then we were docking and then we were driving and then we were climbing the stairs in the Parliament Building.

"May I help you?" a grey-haired receptionist asked.

"Yes," my mom said, peering over the top of the large carton she was carrying, "I'm Joan Shapiro and I have an appointment with Premier —"

"Oh, yes, the sculptor," the receptionist said, breaking into a smile. "We've been expecting you. Right this way." She opened a door with PREMIER'S OFFICE etched in gold letters on the glass.

"Mr. Premier, Ms. Shapiro to see you."

"Joan, come in, come in." Premier Sherman greeted us at the door. He took the box from my mother, then dipped a little and set it carefully on his desk. "Boy, she's no lightweight, is she?"

My mom introduced him to my dad and Peggy and me. He looked about my dad's age, though he wasn't as bald. He had reading glasses on the end of his nose, which he pushed on top of his head. There were deep lines creasing his forehead, but they went away when he smiled.

"So good to meet all of you," he said. "You're an artist as well, I take it?" he said to my dad.

"Yes, Mr. Premier —"

"Just call me Jack."

"He makes wonderful stained glass windows," my mom told him.

"Really." He looked admiringly at my dad. "I'd like to see some of those sometime. Unfortunately — for my personal finances, that is — my wife has a thing about stained glass. As well as goddesses."

He and my parents laughed.

"And you, young lady," he said, bending down to me, "are you an artist, too?"

"No — sir — Jack."

He chuckled. "Hey, I like that. 'Sir Jack.'"

My mom put her hand on my shoulder. "No, Jack, Starshine has other interests — unusual interests — which you might like to hear about later."

Huh? What did she say that for?

"And you," he said, bending down further, "must be Peggy, right?"

"Right." She gave him the cute look. One pigtail bounced.

He gazed musingly at her. "You look familiar, though I can't say —"

Peggy whirled around. KITTEN KRUNCHIES was emblazoned on the back of her jacket.

"Of course! You're the famous Kitten Krunchies girl."

"And the Biskittens and Kitty-Vites and Kitten Kritters girl, too."

"Wow. What a talented family." He moved over toward his desk. "Now … " He put his hand on the box. "Do you think … " His fingers thrummed and an eager smile twitched at his mouth. "Can I see her now?"

"Of course," my mom said. She slit open the tape on top of the box, pulled out scrunched up balls of newspaper, and she and my dad lifted out the sculpture.

"Put her right here," Jack said, pointing to a coffee table near the window. Made of dark wood carved in an old-fashioned design, it was just wide enough to hold the sculpture. "I told you I had the perfect spot."

My parents put it down and the Premier came over and gazed at his new sculpture. It was the first time I'd seen it, too, so I took a good look. Demeter was a chubby goddess, shaped like an eggplant, rounder at the bottom. She was leaning on her elbow in kind of a lazy pose, with her legs, which looked suspiciously like zucchinis — I knew I'd seen a zucchini in that drawing! — stretched out to the side. There was a satisfied smile on her face — probably because it had been a good harvest. Her lap was filled with apples and corn and potatoes and cherries and turnips and beans. Her hair was long and flowing, with carrots in it — as if some strands had turned into carrots, or maybe the carrots had turned into hair, I couldn't tell which. It reminded me of that poem where all the birds built their nests in that guy's beard, just as he feared.

Having carrots in your hair was strange enough, but what was stranger was that Demeter's free hand, the one that wasn't propping up her head, was sticking out, palm up, forming a kind of cup. What was that for? Was she begging? Asking somebody to read her palm? Collecting rainwater?

The Premier walked all around Demeter, leaning in to peer closely from time to time. I felt my mom stiffen. Finally, I guess she couldn't stand it anymore.

"Well?"

"Well!" he said, turning to her. "Joan, she's wonderful! She's perfect!"

My mom heaved a sigh of relief.

"She captures the fertility, the joy of the harvest. Such abundance. Such bounty. Such yummy food. Now I only hope she blesses my garden with good luck."

My mom beamed.

"But, I must ask you … " He pointed at the cupped hand. At least I wasn't the only one who didn't get it.

"A plant holder, of course," my mom said. "Since you love gardening, I figured you must have potted plants in your office —" She broke off and looked around. "There!" She seized a small spider plant sitting on a bookshelf and placed it in Demeter's hand. "See?"

"Now she's perfect," the Premier said. "How ingenious." He shook my mom's hand again. "You've brightened up my office, Joan. I can't thank you enough."

"I'm so glad you like her."

"Like her? I love her. You've outdone yourself, you really have." He patted Demeter on the head, then shook all of our hands again. "Thank you for coming." As he was shaking hands, he glanced at his appointment book, which lay open on his desk. I glanced at it, too. There was writing on every line. Boy, he was a busy guy.

I heard some voices in the hall. Must be whoever he was meeting with next. My mom flashed my dad a look. Why weren't we leaving? The Premier clearly wanted us to go. We were going to make him late for his next appointment.

"Uh, Jack, there is one more thing," my mom said.

"What? Oh … uh … yes?"

"Well," my mom said, darting a look at me, then my dad, then back at the Premier, "remember when I said before that my daughter has other interests? Unusual interests? Well, she does. Spiders, to be precise."

"Spiders?"

"Spiders."

"Mom!" What on earth was she doing?

"Yes. And Starshine has been trying to have a particular spider, the *Araneus vampiricus*, or fanged vampire spider, named the Provincial Arachnid of British Columbia."

How did she know? But more to the point, why would he care? "Mom," I said again, yanking her sleeve, trying to drag her out of there.

"Provincial Arachnid? As in the Provincial Symbols?"

He sounded so doubtful, I got mad. Forgetting, for a moment, who I was talking to, I said, "We have a Provincial Tartan, for goodness sake. I don't see why we can't have a Provincial Arachnid."

Then I wanted to die. What was I thinking, snapping at the Premier of British Columbia?

But to my surprise, he looked at me and nodded. "You're absolutely right," he said. "Why can't we?" To my mom, he said, "Go on."

The rumblings in the hall grew louder. Sounded like the Premier's next group of guests was getting restless.

"Starshine found out that you have to get three thousand signatures on a petition to have something named a Provincial Symbol," my mom said.

How did she know this?

"Three thousand? Boy, that's a lot," the Premier said.

"You're telling me," I said.

"Well?" he said to my mom.

"Well, quite unbeknownst to Pete and me, Starshine has been beavering away all summer, collecting signatures. We don't know how many she's collected, or how she's collected them, for that matter, but I think it's safe to say that she hasn't quite got three thousand."

Yeah, no kidding, I thought. Not quite. End of story. Let's get out of here.

"Yes?" The Premier looked confused, as if wondering why my mom was telling him this. So was I. I didn't have enough signatures, so why was she wasting his time?

My mom smiled mysteriously. "But last night we got a phone call. A very surprising phone call."

She opened the Premier's office door. And in walked Julie, Glynnis, Roxanne, Priya, Frannie and Miranda.

# Chapter Eighteen

I thought my heart had stopped. But it couldn't have stopped, because it was hammering like a woodpecker's bill on a hollow tree.

I couldn't look at Julie. I couldn't not look at her. I didn't know where to look. I looked at her hands. They were full of papers.

What were the papers? What was she doing here? What were they all doing here?

I looked at the others. They were grinning and giggling and squirming. Just like when I saw them last, when they were laughing at me. Was this some further humiliation? Another betrayal? I felt my skin flush with anger.

Julie stepped forward and handed my mom the stack of papers. "Here you go, Mrs. Shapiro. We got 1,802."

One thousand eight hundred and two *what*?

"Ms. Shapiro … ?" the Premier said.

"Yes, Mr. Premier. To continue. Starshine's best friend, Julie Wong, called me last night. She told me … "

At the words "best friend," my stomach clenched and I nearly missed what my mom was saying.

" ... collected 1,802 signatures — without Starshine knowing a thing about it. And here they are!" She handed him the pile.

One thousand eight hundred and two *signatures*?

Oh my God.

I couldn't grasp it. All summer, I'd been thinking about nothing but signatures. But now, faced with 1,802 of them, I couldn't get my head around it. My friends had collected them ... for me?

I looked at Julie. Then at Glynnis, leaning on her crutches ... at Roxanne, smiling beneath her freckles ... at Frannie, practically squirming with excitement ... at Priya, her face serious and expectant ... at Miranda, beaming at me ...

And back at Julie. Her face said, Aren't you surprised? It said, I'm not sure if you deserve it. It said, What is going on with you?

I felt sick to my stomach. She'd collected signatures for me. Without my knowing. Without saying a word. They all had. All summer they must have been ... While I was ... How could I have thought ... ?

My head reeled.

"You mean ... you ... all of you ... " Then I thought of something. I turned to the others. "How did you know?"

"Julie, of course," Glynnis said.

Julie. Of course. "At my —"

"At your party. Right."

Oh my God.

I shook my head in bewilderment. "But how? How did you do it?"

"We bugged everybody we knew and we just kept bugging them until they signed," Roxanne said, and they all laughed.

"Roxanne's very good at bugging," Miranda said, and they laughed again.

I looked from face to face.

"I got everybody at Camp Crescent Moon," Roxanne said. "Even Ruth!"

"I corralled people at a CP conference," Glynnis said. "Wouldn't let them get away without signing — wheelchair or no wheelchair."

"I got everybody who works at my mom's TV studio," Miranda said.

"I got everybody at my gymnastics club," Frannie added.

"I got everybody who goes to my swimming pool," Priya said.

"I hit Chinatown," Julie said. "Everybody signed. In Chinese and English."

I was still stunned. All this time I'd thought they were making fun of me, laughing behind my back, keeping secrets from me, and instead they were helping me. Planning to surprise me.

"You're not going to believe what I thought," I whispered, ashamed. I covered my face with my hands. Tears welled up in my eyes. I struggled not to cry in front of everyone. If Julie knew what I'd thought, she'd really be hurt — hurt that I could have thought she'd do all those things.

Then another thing hit me. In spite of everything — in spite of the fact that I'd accused her of being phony, of stealing my friends, of being mean, of plotting behind my back, of ditching me for new friends — she'd still gone out and collected the signatures for me.

I looked at Julie. "Why?" I said. "Why'd you do it?"

She looked straight back at me. "'Cause you're my best friend. Even if you were being a jerk, you're still my best friend. That's what best friends do. I'd said I would help. Did you think I would let you down?"

That did it. I threw my arms around her and bawled. "Oh, Julie, I'm sorry, I'm so sorry." I sobbed. She cried, too, holding me. Then I thought of how I'd wronged the others, too, with my suspicions. "I'm sorry, you guys, I'm really sorry … "

"What's she sorry about?" Roxanne said.

"Beats me," Frannie said.

I cried so hard Premier Sherman offered me his handkerchief. "Oh, I couldn't, Mr. — Jack —" I blew my nose in it. "I'll wash it, Mr. Premier, I promise." I laughed, then cried some more.

The Premier looked bewildered. "Forgive me, Joan, I have nothing against a good cry now and then, but what does all this have to do with me?"

"Well, you see, Jack, I don't know how many signatures Starshine has, but when Julie called last night and said she had 1,802, I thought, well, that's nearly two-thirds. Maybe that gives Starshine enough."

"Well, let's ask her, then." The Premier looked at me. "How many do you have, Starshine?"

I was already slipping my backpack off my shoulders. I drew out the stack, handed it to him and said "1,194. Quick, somebody, pencil and paper."

The Premier was already scribbling. "That totals 2,996."

Four short.

Everybody in the room groaned. But before I could think what to do, my mom grabbed a pen. "Here, Pete, let's sign."

"Can we do this, as the petitioner's parents? Isn't that kind of like insider trading?"

"Nonsense," my mother said. "We're both citizens of British Columbia." They signed.

Now we had 2,998.

Two short.

All eyes turned to Premier Sherman. He held up his hands. "I know that's heartbreakingly close, but I really can't interfere in matters of protocol. It wouldn't be fair, you see —"

I couldn't breathe. The whole thing lost because of two signatures!

Then … an idea.

"There's one thing my mom forgot to tell you, Mr. Premier," I said. My heart was pounding.

"Yes? What's that?"

"The fanged vampire spider eats slugs."

"It — WHAT? Did you say it eats slugs?"

"Yes, sir."

He jumped to his feet. "Why didn't you say so in the first

place? I HATE SLUGS! I DESPISE SLUGS! I LOATHE SLUGS!" He punched a button on his telephone. "Ms. Joseph, would you please ask Jane Smith of Protocol and Events to pop into my office for a moment?"

"Certainly, Mr. Premier."

We waited. The Premier paced.

A rap on the door, then a black face with short curly black hair poked round it. "You wanted to see me, Mr. Premier?"

"Yes, come in, Ms. Smith. I want you to meet a remarkable young woman. Ms. Smith, may I present Starshine Shapiro?"

She turned, her eyes sweeping across the crowd. I stepped forward.

"You're Starshine?"

"You're Jane?"

We beamed at each other.

"You did it?"

"Yup."

"Way to go, Starshine!" She pumped my hand.

"You know about this, Ms. Smith?" Premier Sherman asked

She turned around with a big grin. "Yes, Mr. Premier. I knew she was going to try, anyway. Now, what did you want to see me about?"

"Ah, yes." Premier Sherman rested his hand on Demeter's head. "Tell me, Ms. Smith, is there anything in the rules of Protocol that says a Premier can't sign a petition, even if that petition concerns, say, the Provincial Symbols?"

"No, Mr. Premier."

"Good. And is there anything that would prevent a member of the Premier's staff from signing?"

"No, Mr. Premier."

"Very good." He handed her a pen. "If you would be so kind as to sign here." He pointed to the last petition sheet. She signed her name. He took the pen from her and signed on the last line. Line three thousand. Premier Jack Sherman.

It took one final moment to sink in.

Then I burst into tears and burst out laughing at the same time. I started jumping up and down, right in the Premier's office, and soon Julie and Roxanne and Priya and Frannie and Miranda were jumping up and down, too, and Glynnis was banging her crutches on the floor, and the Premier's floor was shaking, and secretaries and janitors and Members of the Legislative Assembly were peeking around the door to see what on earth was going on, and we were all laughing and crying and yelling, "We did it! We did it! We did it!"

# Chapter Nineteen

Julie and I sat on the outside ferry deck with our backs against a stairwell wall. The wind whipped our hair into our faces. Julie drew her legs inside the circle of her arms and waited.

I was scared. When I told her, she'd be hurt. She might even get mad at me. I took a deep breath. "Remember at my party, when you guys were talking in the living room — I wasn't there, I'd just come back from the Ice Cream Pagoda with Peggy — and you said something about a chair being knocked over and making a big noise and being a klutz and how funny it was?"

"Yeah."

"Well …" I gulped. "I thought you were telling them about my Wizard of Oz audition. When I screwed up."

"You what!"

"Well …"

"Star!" She looked offended. "How could you? I'd never tell anybody about that!"

"Well, I didn't know. And what was I supposed to think? What other chair could you possibly have been talking about?"

"*Your* chair, you idiot!"

"What? Which one?"

"The one in your room.

"Huh?"

"Your desk chair."

"What were you doing with my desk chair?" I was totally confused.

"It was when I rushed back from the Ice Cream Pagoda. Remember?"

"Yeah, I remember. I couldn't figure out what you were in such a hurry for."

"I was in a hurry to steal the instructions for the petitions before you got back, so I could make copies and send them to everybody."

"Huh?"

"Star, I knew that you and I weren't going to get 3,000 signatures by ourselves. There was no way. So while your camp friends and I were sitting eating our ice cream, I got a brain-storm — to get all of them to help. So I asked them, and of course they said yes."

"But — but why didn't you tell me?"

"BECAUSE IT WAS GOING TO BE A SURPRISE!"

"Oh," I said in a small voice. "So that's what 'don't tell' meant."

"Yeah."

So there *had* been a secret. It just wasn't what I'd thought it was. "But what about the chair?"

"Well, I was going through your desk and I knew you'd be back any minute. I was in a panic to find the instructions and I knocked over your chair and it made a racket and I was afraid you'd hear it and you'd want to know what I was doing rooting around in your desk and then it wouldn't be a surprise!"

"Oh."

There was a pause.

"Star, how could you think that?"

"Well," I said huffily, "I didn't know what you were up to. There's only one chair that's been knocked over that I know of, and I did it. So what else could I think? And then everybody kept looking at me and snickering, so I figured you'd told them."

"Star!"

"And then they asked you to do your *Wizard of Oz* song, and I thought you all were rubbing it in."

"Star, we wouldn't!"

"And then, when I saw Roxanne and Frannie and Priya and Miranda at the Ice Cream Pagoda, I knew they were up to something, and I thought they were plotting something about me —"

"Star, for goodness sake!"

"And then when I saw you at the rollerblading rink —" I stopped short. "You were gathering signatures."

"Of course!"

"I thought — you wouldn't believe what I thought." I took a breath. "I'm really sorry, Jule."

"You should be," she said sharply. Then more gently, "You should have known, Star."

"I know. I was crazy. Temporary insanity. That's the only explanation."

She smiled briefly, then fell silent. I could tell she was thinking over everything I'd said. "Well … " she said slowly, "I can see where you'd be hurt if you thought I *had* told."

I waited.

"And I can see where you *might* think they were laughing at you."

I waited.

"And I can see where you *might* think we were keeping secrets from you."

I waited.

"But you should have known I'd *never* tell anyone about your audition!"

"I know, but — oh, Jule, I got this idea in my head — it was a crazy idea, I know that now — but at the time it seemed to make sense, and everything seemed to fit and — well, I just let myself get carried away."

"Never, ever, ever."

"I know that, Jule. I do — now. Really."

Silence.

"Really, really. A hundred times really."

She shot me a smile. A real smile. The first good old Julie smile I'd seen all day. All summer. "That's the last time I plan a surprise for you."

"I sure hope so. I don't think I could live through another one."

We giggled. The mad feeling started draining away. I took

a deep breath, feeling as though a huge weight had been lifted off me. We sat for a minute, just enjoying being together again.

"You nut," she said fondly.

"Jule … you're the best friend a friend ever had."

"Aw, shucks."

"No, really."

"You're not so bad either … except when you're being dopey."

"Well, yeah."

"And dense."

"That, too."

"And stubborn."

"Hey!"

We laughed, gave each other a huge hug and went back inside. The others were squished together on the floor at the very front of the ferry, beneath the big windows. They looked up.

"Did you figure out what she was sorry about?" Roxanne asked Julie.

"Yeah."

"And are you done being sorry?" she asked me.

"Yeah."

"Good. Sit down and join the party."

Good old Roxanne, bossy as ever. Julie and I squeezed in. Everybody was laughing and joking and it felt so great just to sit with them and be part of it and not be mad or hurt anymore. Just to be with my friends.

Two weeks later, I stood with hundreds of other people in the Chamber of Provincial Symbols. It was crowded. Mobbed, in fact. People in suits and dresses were chatting and giving each other little rectangular cards. Other people in black-and-white uniforms were circulating with glasses of wine and sparkly water and trays of little crispy things. I had no idea what they were, but they were delicious and I ate lots of them.

I squeezed to the back of the room. The mural had been completely redone. Under the title PROVINCIAL ARACHNID was a picture of the *Araneus vampiricus*, red and yellow stripes and all. It was nestled between the Official Mineral Emblem and the Provincial Tartan. "*The Araneus vampiricus*, or fanged vampire spider," read the inscription, "was chosen by the people of British Columbia as their Provincial Arachnid. The *Araneus vampiricus* is known for its colourful markings, its razor-sharp black fangs and its unusual diet, which consists entirely of slippery, slimy slugs."

Julie squeezed in beside me. We admired the mural together.

"We did it, Star."

"Yeah, we did — though there were times when I really didn't think it would happen."

"What do you mean, not happen?" a voice said.

Julie and I turned. It was Nona, together with Rob.

"Of course it was going to happen," Nona went on. "We just had to hang in there and not give up. Keep pushing. Hold the line. Hold the fort. And we did. We showed 'em, didn't we?"

"We sure did," Julie said, looking at Nona in awe.

Nona had that gleam in her eye. "And you know what I think, Starshine? I think we should take on another fight. All of us, Rob and me and all your friends. With Rob doing his thing on the computer, and the rest of us out there hustling, we can't lose. You got any other spiders you want to save, Starshine?"

Before I could answer, Rob put up his hand. "N-n-n-NO! No way. Don't even think about it."

"But Rob," I said, "I thought you were *into* doing stuff now."

"Yeah, you said it was fun," Nona added.

"Yeah, but now I'm practising."

"Practising for what?"

"For when school starts. I can't have my teachers and everybody thinking I'm a go-getter kind of guy. They'll start piling the work on, expecting me to do it all. Besides, I have an image to keep up." He shook his head. "Sorry, but I'm going back to being a couch potato. I lost my grip for a while, but I'll get it back, I know I will, if I just relax and take it easy … " He wandered off, breathing deeply.

"We'll see about that," Nona said, and went off after him.

Julie and I laughed.

"He hasn't got a chance," I said.

Premier Sherman called everyone to order and we gathered in front of the mural. "Ladies and gentlemen, we are gathered here today to mark a very auspicious occasion. Today, British Columbia takes its place as a leader among provinces. Today, British Columbia gives gardeners a reason to rejoice. Today, British Columbia adopts the *Araneus vampiricus* as its Provincial Arachnid."

There was a smattering of applause.

The Premier went on, "Ladies and gentlemen, don't let anyone tell you that young people can't make a difference, because they sure can. We would not be here today, were it not for the efforts of one plucky, determined, imaginative girl. Ladies and gentlemen, I give you Starshine Bliss Shapiro!"

Huge applause. Lightbulbs flashing. Murmurs of surprise. People craning their necks to see — me.

"Thank you, Mr. — er — Jack — uh — Premier — er — Sherman. I'm really happy it all worked out. And that the fanged vampire spider is going to be British Columbia's Provincial Arachnid. It deserves it. It's a great spider. It has beautiful yellow markings on the underside of its abdomen — well, you probably don't want to hear about that."

There were a few giggles.

"One more thing," I said. "Premier Sherman said 'the efforts of one girl.' But that's not true. *I* got the idea — and a lot of people said it was a crazy idea —"

More laughter.

"But I didn't do it myself. A whole lot of people chipped in and made it happen. And I just want to say that I couldn't have done it —"

I shifted position so I could see everybody who had helped. Taking my time, I looked each one in the face: my mom and dad and Peggy, and Glynnis, Roxanne, Frannie, Priya and Miranda, and Rob and Nona, and Ms. Fung, and Gertie and Flossie and Doug, and Jane Smith and Premier Sherman, and, most of all, Julie.

"— without the help of my wonderful, marvelous, fabulous, true-blue friends!"

## About the Author

Ellen Schwartz lives with her family in Burnaby, British Columbia, where she works as a freelance writer and teaches courses in writing for children. She has an MFA in Creative Writing from the University of British Columbia and is an avid reader and hiker. She confesses to being "still something of a hippie" — not unlike Starshine Shapiro's parents.

# POLESTAR

An Imprint of Raincoast Books

Polestar Books, an imprint of Raincoast Books, takes pride in creating books that introduce discriminating readers to exciting writers. These independent voices illuminate our histories and engage our imaginations.

## More Books for Young Readers from Polestar:

*Starshine!* • Ellen Schwartz

A Canadian Children's Book Centre "Our Choice" book. "This lively and funny novel is a winner." — *Quill & Quire*

ISBN 0-919591-24-8 • $8.95 CDN/$5.95 USA

*Starshine at Camp Crescent Moon* • Ellen Schwartz

"Through comic details, Schwartz has crafted an easy-read winner." — *CCL*

ISBN 0919591-02-7 • $8.95 CDN/$5.95 USA

*Starshine on TV* • Ellen Schwartz

Nominated for the Silver Birch Award. "Schwartz has succeeded in creating completely believable, sympathetic and interesting characters who care deeply for each other and the world." — *Canadian Materials*

ISBN 0-896095-13-5 • $8.95 CDN/$5.95 USA

*Witch's Fang* • Heather Kellerhals-Stewart

Three teens risk their lives in this mountain-climbing adventure.

ISBN 1-55192-368-8 • $8.95 CDN/$6.95 USA